"Angie...?"

Angie swallowed hard on the thickness in her throat. "I think you owe me one favor, Leo. I want you to promise me that as soon as this wretched visit is over you'll fix me up with a job somewhere."

"You won't need a job. Your future is already assured. I will keep you..."

"Nobody keeps me, Leo."

"My offer is open at any time you want to take it up."

She spun away, jumpy as a cat on hot bricks. "You're astonishingly persistent."

Raw desire blazed in his bold dark eyes. "Hungry...very, very hungry," he corrected her.

LYNNE GRAHAM was born in Northern Ireland and has been a keen romance reader since her teens. She is very happily married, with an understanding husband who has learned to cook since she started to write! Her five children keep her on her toes. She has a very large old English sheepdog, which knocks everything over, and two cats. When time allows, Lynne is a keen gardener.

Books by Lynne Graham

HARLEQUIN PRESENTS
1864—PRISONER OF PASSION
1875—THE DESERT BRIDE
1888—SECOND-TIME BRIDE
1908—THE HEAT OF PASSION
1937—MISTRESS AND MOTHER
1961—THE SECRET WIFE
1971—THE RELUCTANT HUSBAND

LYNNE GRAHAM

The Winter Bride

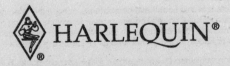

HARLEQUIN®

TORONTO • NEW YORK • LONDON
AMSTERDAM • PARIS • SYDNEY • HAMBURG
STOCKHOLM • ATHENS • TOKYO • MILAN • MADRID
PRAGUE • WARSAW • BUDAPEST • AUCKLAND

ISBN 0-373-11989-5

THE WINTER BRIDE

First North American Publication 1998.

CHAPTER ONE

'A RISE...you're actually *asking* us for a *rise*?' Claudia looked at the younger woman with shocked and incredulous eyes, much as if the girl had asked for a half-share in the house. 'I think we're more than generous as it is. You have your salary as well as free board and lodging, and do please remember that we're keeping *two* of you!'

Although Angie was severely embarrassed by that response, she forced herself to continue. 'I often work six days a week and I baby-sit several nights as well...'

Her persistence fired angry colour in the elegant brunette's cheeks. 'I can't believe that we're even having this conversation. You do some housework and you mind the children. Why shouldn't you baby-sit? You have to sit in every night to look after Jake...surely you're not expecting us to pay extra for what you'd be doing anyway? I don't know how you can be so ungrateful after all we've done for you—'

'I'm just finding it very hard to make ends meet,' Angie slotted in tightly, a deep sense of humiliation creeping over her.

'Well, I'm sure I don't know what you're doing with your salary when you have all your bills paid for you,' her employer retorted very drily. 'What I do know is that my husband, George, will be extremely shocked when I tell him about this demand of yours.'

'It wasn't a demand,' Angie countered tensely. 'It was a request.'

'Request refused, then,' Claudia told her sharply as she stalked to the kitchen door. 'I'm very annoyed about this and *very* disappointed in you, Angie. You have a really cushy job here. Gosh, I wish someone would pay *me* to stay home and fill the dishwasher! We treat you and Jake like part of our family. We kept you on when you were pregnant...and let me assure you that not one of our friends would even have *considered* retaining a pregnant and un-married au pair in their home!'

Angie said nothing. There was nothing more to say un-less she was prepared to risk Claudia's explosive temper and the threat of dismissal. No au pair worked the hours Angie did. But then she wasn't an au pair even though Claudia persisted in calling her one. She might have come to the Dickson family in that guise, accepting the equivalent of pocket money in place of a salary, but slowly and surely her hours had crept up until she was doing the full-time job of a housekeeper and childminder. At the time she had been so grateful to still have a roof over her head that she had made no objection.

But then she had been very naive when she was preg-nant. She had seen the Dicksons as a temporary staging post, had fondly imagined that once she had her baby she would be able to move on to better-paid employment and build up her life again. But piece by piece that confidence had faded once she appreciated the cost of child care and the even greater cost of renting accommodation in a city as expensive as London. Ultimately it had come down to a choice between continuing to work for the Dicksons and moving out to live on welfare.

'We'll say no more about this,' Claudia murmured gra-ciously from the doorway, well aware that silence meant that she had won. 'Do you think you could start putting the children in the bath now? It is half past six, and they're so dreadfully noisy when they get over-tired.'

By the time Angie had got the children to bed it was well after eight, and George and Claudia had long since gone out to dine. Six-year-old Sophia and the four-year-old twins, Benedict and Oscar, were lovely children—very rich in material possessions but pretty much starved of parental attention. Their father was a circuit judge, regularly away from home, and their mother a high-powered business-woman, who only rarely left her office before seven in the evening.

They had a spacious, beautifully furnished home and a Porsche and a Range Rover, but Claudia was so mean with money that she had had a pay meter installed on the gas fire in Angie's room over the attached garage. Since the room had no central heating, and had originally been cheaply converted only for the purpose of storage space, it was freezing cold in winter.

The doorbell shrilled while Angie was ensuring that the only part of her son exposed to that chilly air was the crown of his dark, curly head. She tucked the duvet round Jake in a rush and hurtled through the door that connected with the bedroom corridor to race downstairs before the bell could go again and wake Sophia, who was a very light sleeper.

Thrusting back the wild tangle of platinum pale hair that had flown round her anxious face, she pressed the intercom. 'Who is it?' she asked breathlessly.

'Angie…?'

In severe shock, Angie fell back from the intercom. Like sand on silk, and splinteringly, shatteringly sexy, the voice had a husky Greek accent that roughened every vowel sound. It had been over two years since she had heard that masculine drawl and recognition filled her with sheer, blind panic.

The doorbell went again in a short, impatient burst.

'Please don't do that…you'll wake the children!' Angie gasped into the intercom.

'Angie…open the door,' Leo drawled flatly.

'I—I *can't*…I'm not allowed to open it when I'm alone in the house at night,' Angie muttered with feverish relief in telling the truth. 'I don't know what you want or how you found me, and I don't care. Just go away!'

In answer, Leo hit the doorbell again.

With a groan of frustration, Angie flew out into the

porch, wrenched back the curtains, undid the bolts and the chain and dragged open the front door.

'Thank you,' Leo responded with icy precision.

Poleaxed by his very presence, Angie gaped at him, her pulse thudding wildly at the foot of her throat. 'You still can't come in…'

A winged ebony brow lifted with hauteur. 'Don't be ridiculous.'

Involuntarily, Angie gazed up into eyes the colour of a wild and stormy night, and a shiver of shaken reaction ran through her. Leo Demetrios in the flesh. He was standing close enough to touch on the Dicksons' doorstep, six feet three inches of daunting sophistication and devastating masculinity. Broad shoulders filled out his superbly cut dinner jacket, perfectly tailored black trousers accentuating lean hips and long, long legs. The overhead security light delineated every carved angle of his savagely handsome features and glinted over his thick blue-black hair, but she still couldn't believe that he was really, genuinely there in front of her.

'You can't come in,' she said again, running damp palms down over her faded jeans.

'Angie…I wanna drink…I'm thirsty,' Sophia mumbled sleepily from the stairs.

Angie jumped and spun round to rush back into the dimly lit hall. 'Go back to bed and I'll bring you one up…'

Leo stepped into the porch and quietly closed the door. Angie turned again, giving him a dismayed and pleading look, but she didn't want to speak to him and alert the sleepy Sophia to the presence of a forbidden visitor. Biting her lip in frantic frustration, she left him there and sped into the kitchen to pour a glass of water and took it upstairs. Claudia and George had only gone out for a quick meal and they might be on their way back even now. They would be absolutely outraged if they found her entertaining a strange man in their home.

Her thoughts in complete turmoil as she struggled to understand why Leo should have sought her out, she settled Sophia and started hurriedly down the stairs again. Mercifully, Leo was still standing in the hall. She wouldn't have been surprised to find him installed on one of the leather sofas in the drawing room. People ran out red carpets when Leo condescended to visit; they didn't keep him on the doorstep or leave him to hover in the hall. His hugely successful global electronics empire generated immense wealth, and he wielded formidable power and influence in the business world.

Belatedly encountering Leo's raking and uninhibited scrutiny of her slender but shapely figure, Angie faltered on the last step of the stairs. His spectacular dark, deep-set eyes smouldered as they skimmed up from the surprisingly full thrust of her breasts to strike her own eyes in direct collision. She ran out of breath and mobility simultaneously, throat closing over, heart pounding so suffocatingly fast behind her ribcage that she felt dizzy.

'I won't keep you long,' Leo informed her with a sardonic smile.

'What are you doing here?' Angie practically whispered, struggling to surmount that momentary loss of concentration and finding it almost impossible until a stark current of foreboding assailed her and her bright blue eyes widened in sudden dismay. 'Are you here because of my father? Is he ill or something?'

Leo frowned. 'To my knowledge, Brown is in good health.'

Angie flushed brick-red, utterly mortified by the spurt of fear that had prompted her foolish enquiry. She perfectly understood Leo's brief look of disconcertion. No doubt it would be a cold day in hell before Leo Demetrios stooped to act as a messenger boy for one of his grandfather's servants!

In an awkward invitation and sudden revolt against Claudia's rigid rules, she pressed open the door of the little

TV room. 'We can talk in here,' she said stiffly, striving desperately for an air of normality.

But oh, dear heaven, that was an impossible challenge with Jake enjoying the sleep of the innocent upstairs and Leo behaving like a coldly polite stranger. Maybe he was afraid that if he was friendly she might throw herself at him again, Angie thought in sudden, cringing horror. Her colour fluctuating wildly, she dropped her head, but cruelly humiliating memories still bombarded her like guided missiles finding an easy target.

She had been foolishly obsessed with Leo for more years than she now cared to recall. And she had not been the sort of dreaming teenager who sat around simply hoping for a miracle to occur. At nineteen, she had plotted and planned like crazy to get her chance with Leo. She had broken every rule in the book to catch him. She had forgotten who he was and who she was in the chase. And, at the end of the day, she had got very much what she had asked for—Leo had dumped her so hard and fast, her head had spun.

The silence pounded and pulsed.

Nervously, Angie glanced up to find Leo watching her again. Involuntarily, she was entrapped, pulses quickening, skin dampening. Colour drenched her complexion. She ran a nervous hand through the long hair falling round her face, and moved her head to toss it back out of her way. Leo's gaze followed the rippling motion of that cascade of pale, shining strands, increasing her self-consciousness. Then dense black lashes veiled his burnished dark eyes, and his beautifully shaped, sensual mouth hardened again.

'How did you find out where I lived?' Angie asked in a jerky rush, because the silence was unbearable. She did not have his nerves of steel and self-discipline.

'My grandfather asked me to trace you—'

Her fine brows pleated. '*Wallace?*' she broke in incredulously, referring to his English grandfather whose daughter had married Leo's father, a Greek shipping magnate.

'I'm here only to pass on an invitation,' Leo imparted

smoothly. 'Wallace would like you to spend Christmas with him.'

'Christmas?' Angie parroted weakly.

'He wants to become acquainted with his great grandson.'

That final, shattering announcement left Angie gaping at him in even deeper shock. Her knees threatening to give way, she groped her passage down into an armchair. Leo *knew* she had been pregnant? Leo *knew* that she now had a child? She had never dreamt that Wallace Neville might share that secret with his grandson.

And now Wallace actually wanted to *meet* Jake? Yet Wallace had forcefully urged her to terminate her pregnancy over two years ago. The news that the butler's daughter had been impregnated by one of his grandsons had so appalled him, he had been apoplectic with rage. An unapologetic snob with a horror of scandal, he had been eager to facilitate Angie's departure from Deveraux Court that very same day.

'Old men feel their mortality.' Leo's dark eyes rested unreadably on her stunningly beautiful face. 'And, frankly, curiosity seems to be killing him. Obviously it will be in your best interests to grovel gratefully in the face of his generosity.'

'Grovel?' Angie echoed in complete bewilderment.

Leo's appraisal became grim, his mouth twisting. 'I know about the deal you made with Wallace, Angie. I know the *whole* story.'

Angie stiffened in disbelief, lashes dropping low on fiercely anxious eyes. 'I haven't a clue what you're talking about.'

'You know very well what I'm talking about,' Leo countered steadily.

Her slim fingers closed together and clenched. She studied the carpet until it blurred, her stomach churning with sick apprehension.

'The thefts, Angie,' Leo supplied without remorse. 'Wallace caught you in the act and you confessed.'

Her head flew up, anguish and resentment mingling in her stricken face. 'He promised that he would never tell anyone!'

She wanted to die right there and then. Wallace had promised, Wallace had promised faithfully—and by 'anyone' Angie had meant specifically *Leo*. She could not bear the knowledge that Leo thought she had been the thief, responsible for stealing several small but valuable *objets d'art* from Deveraux Court where her father and stepmother both worked and lived.

'Angie, nothing disappeared after your departure. That fact rather spoke for itself. Wallace had little hope of keeping the identity of the culprit under wraps.'

'So my father must know as well,' she mumbled, mortified pain clogging up her vocal cords as she made that final leap in understanding.

'I've never discussed the matter with him,' Leo retorted crisply.

In all her life, Angie knew she had never tasted greater humiliation. Her shaken eyes stung fiercely. She studied Leo's hand-stitched Italian leather shoes and hated him for believing and accepting that she had been the thief. And, even more cruelly, throwing that conviction in her face. Was this why he had referred to Jake as if her child were nothing whatsoever to do with him?

Was her supposed dishonesty so offensive that Leo could not bring himself to acknowledge that she was the mother of his child? she asked herself in growing bewilderment. What had Leo said? *Wallace* wanted to become acquainted with his great-grandson. Had that been Leo's way of telling her that he himself had no intention of taking the smallest interest in Jake? She found that she couldn't think straight because nothing Leo had yet said had made any kind of sense to her.

'I want you to leave,' Angie confided shakily. 'I didn't ask you to come looking for me.'

'That's an irrational response and you'll think better of it within a very short space of time,' Leo asserted crushingly. 'Wallace would have called the police if you hadn't told him that you were pregnant. You were fortunate to escape a prison sentence. Those thefts took place over a long period. They were neither opportunistic nor the result of someone succumbing to sudden temptation.'

Briefly, Angie closed her aching eyes in a spasm of bitter regret. When in the heat of the moment she had confessed to something she hadn't done, she had been bolstered by the belief that she was protecting someone she loved and that, in any case, she herself had nothing more to lose. After all, she had already lost Leo, had already accepted that she would have to leave Deveraux Court before her condition became obvious. She had been too proud and too devastated by Leo's rejection to confront him with the consequences of their stolen weekend of passion.

'Wallace is prepared to overlook the past for the sake of your child,' Leo continued levelly.

'My child has a name...and his name is Jake,' Angie told him thinly.

If possible, Leo's rawly handsome features set even harder as he ignored that unasked-for piece of information. 'In your position it would be very foolish to ignore the offer of an olive branch. I believe that Wallace may now be willing to give you financial assistance.'

'I want nothing from any of you.' Hotly flushed and deeply chagrined by the assurance, Angie leapt upright again. 'But I would like to know why Wallace should feel it's *his* responsibility to offer me money!'

Diamond-hard dark eyes assailed hers in icy collision. 'Obviously because his grandson, Drew, has failed to observe his duty to support you both.'

In stark confusion, Angie froze. How was it Drew's duty to support her and Jake? And then finally, and most belatedly, comprehension gripped her, only to leave her drowning in bemusement again. Evidently, Leo was under the impression that his cousin, Drew, had fathered her child. How on earth could he think that? How on earth could *anyone* think that?

Outrage swelled inside Angie until she thought the top of her head might come flying off. In that instant it didn't matter how such a ludicrous misapprehension had come about. Angie was too infuriated by Leo's evident opinion of her morals to concern herself with anything else. So, Leo saw her as a thief *and* a tart. After all, only a fairly promiscuous young woman would have become intimate with *both* of Wallace's grandsons within the space of three months. But Leo was clearly quite happy to believe that she had slept with his cousin after sleeping with him, and no doubt was even more content to believe that responsibility for her illegitimate child could be laid at Drew's door rather than his own.

'Angie, I didn't come here to argue with you or to become involved in personal matters which are frankly nothing to do with me,' Leo drawled in a tone of cool reproof. 'I've issued the invitation on Wallace's behalf, and I haven't got the time to wrangle with you—I have a date, and I'm already running very late.'

For a split second, Angie felt as though he had plunged a knife into her ribs and stabbed her to the heart. *A date?* So the grieving widower was finally back in social circulation... Wow, bully for him! And, naturally, Angie's sordid personal problems were beneath his notice and wholly devoid of interest to him. Indeed, knowing Leo as she did—brutally candid, highly intelligent and uncontrolled only in bed, she enumerated painfully—he had probably been congratulating himself on a narrow escape from severe embarrassment ever since she'd been exposed as the household thief.

'Angie...?' Leo prompted.

She turned round, her perfect features pale and set. As

the bitterness rose inside her, it was the most unbearable
moment of temptation she had ever experienced. She had
a sudden fierce urge to smash Leo's self-possession, punish
him for his deliberate distancing of himself from her pre-
dicament and hurt him, as he was hurting her with the humiliating pretence that they had never been anything to
each other but casual acquaintances.

His hard, dark features were impatient. 'Wallace is expecting you to arrive on Thursday. I assume I can give him
the assurance that you will be accepting his invitation?'

In the unstable hold of a tidal wave of conflicting emotion, Angie tore her pained eyes from the dark, savage
splendour of Leo as he stood there, so effortlessly detached
from her. The anger went out of her at that same moment.

'You've just got to be kidding,' she breathed with a
forced and brittle smile. 'I have no desire to spend Christmas with your grandfather, and I should think he would
have even less desire to spend it with me.'

'I thought you might, at the very least, be tempted by
the possibility of a reconciliation with your own family.'

A humourless laugh was dredged from Angie.
Reconciliation? He didn't know what he was talking about.
She had never had anything but an uneasy and difficult
relationship with her father. Now an unwed mother, and
labelled a thief into the bargain, what possible welcome did
Leo fondly imagine she would receive?

'When I walked out of Deveraux Court...' her throat
thickened, making her voice gruff '...I knew I would never
be walking back. I wasn't sorry to leave and I don't want
to return even for a visit. That whole phase of my life is
behind me now.'

Bold dark eyes scanned her strained profile in exasperation. 'I suppose it was less than tactful of me to mention
the thefts.'

Angie grimaced, willing back tears, determined not to
break down in front of him. 'I would never expect tact or
consideration from you,' she told him helplessly. 'But I

really do object to being patronised. You're out of your
mind if you think I would be willing to go cap in hand to
your grandfather like some pathetic charity case! I've managed fine on my own.'

The very faintest darkening of colour emphasised the
hard slant of Leo's high cheekbones. 'You are working as
a servant...you always swore that you would never do
that.'

Angie flinched, fingernails biting painfully into her
palms. Servant. Not for Leo, surrounded from birth by the
faceless breed, with the more egalitarian label of 'domestic
staff'. As hot pink scored her complexion, she whirled
away from him before she was tempted to slap him for that
most undiplomatic reminder.

'*Theos*... Only the most stupid and selfish pride could
make you refuse so magnanimous an invitation! Wallace
could do a great deal for your son. Think of the child. Why
should he suffer for your mistakes?' Leo demanded abra-
sively. 'It is your duty as a mother to consider his future.'

A raw ripple of pain and fury sizzled through Angie as
she spun back, blue eyes gleaming like sapphires. 'And
what about his father's duty?'

His wide, sensual mouth twisted. 'When you got into bed
with someone as self-centred and irresponsible as Drew,
you must've known that you'd be on your own if anything
went wrong.'

Leo was angry, Angie registered in surprise. Tension
splintered from the fierce cast of his strong features and icy
condemnation glittered in his narrowed gaze. Recognising
that look for what it was, Angie realised that Leo was not
quite as indifferent as he would like to pretend when it
came to his conviction that she had leapt into his cousin's
bed so soon after she had succumbed to him. Bitter amusement filled her at the awareness. *He* hadn't wanted her but
it seemed he hadn't wanted any other man to want her
either.

'Believe it or not, at the time I thought Jake's father was

as steady as a rock,' Angie heard herself admit, tongue-in-cheek. 'I was very much in love with him. In fact I believed he was the very last man likely to leave me in the lurch.'

'You were only nineteen...what did you know then of men or their motivations?' Leo's response was harsh, dismissive, as he glanced with sudden, unconcealed impatience at the thin gold watch on his wrist and strode towards the door. 'I'm afraid I really do have to leave.'

The abruptness of his exit took Angie by surprise. She sped out after him and by then he was already in the porch. As she opened the door, he stared broodingly down at her and, without warning, time slid dangerously back for Angie and served up a disturbingly intimate memory. Leo...responding with shockingly primal dominance to her flirtation, pinning her down in the meadow grass by the lake and crushing her lips beneath his with an explosive, driving hunger that had just blown her away. Embarrassed heat coiled like a burning, aching taunt low in Angie's stomach.

A feverish darkness now overlaid the oblique slant of Leo's cheekbones, but sardonic amusement glittered in his brilliant eyes. He raised a hand and let a long brown forefinger trail gently along the tremulous line of her soft, full mouth, leaving a stunning chain of prickling sensitivity in his wake and sentencing her to shaken stillness. 'You really are wasted in a domestic role, Angie.'

And then, before she could catch her arrested breath, he swung away, striding out into the night air. 'Think over what I have said,' he urged almost carelessly. 'Wallace is keen to meet the child... I'll call tomorrow for your answer.'

'No, don't. There's no point. I've made up my mind and I don't need a night's sleep to consider it,' Angie told him tightly. 'In any case, I couldn't get the time off. The Dicksons have a very busy social calendar over the next ten days, and the house is always full of visitors over Christmas.'

'Can you really have changed so much?' Leo murmured lazily. 'I believed you would walk out of this house like you walked out of my grandfather's without a backward glance.'

Angie flushed furiously. Naturally Leo had assumed that the prospect of money would make her eagerly snatch at his grandfather's invitation, but he had miscalculated. Had *she?* She hadn't told him that Jake was his—had almost done so in anger, but had ultimately remained silent. Why? At the back of her mind lurked the shameful and mortifying recollection that she had told Leo that it was safe to make love to her that weekend…and she had lied, with both purpose and full knowledge of what she was doing.

From the doorway, she watched numbly as Leo strode towards the sleek black Ferrari parked at a careless angle across the paved frontage of the house. Dimly, she registered that she was trembling; reaction was setting in after the terrible tension, sudden coldness biting into her bones.

Headlights suddenly lit up the front garden. Dredged from her introspection, Angie uttered a soundless groan as George's Range Rover raked to a halt.

Claudia virtually leapt from the car. 'What on earth is going on here?' she demanded, casting Leo, who stood in the shadows, a haughty, questioning look, but aiming her ire at Angie as she stalked towards her.

'I called with a message for Angie,' Leo drawled coolly.

'You let a strange man into the house with my children sleeping upstairs?' Claudia ranted in furious attack.

'Darling…' her less volatile husband said rather loudly. 'I don't believe that Mr Demetrios quite qualifies as a strange man.'

'My father works for Leo,' Angie said for the sake of brevity. 'I've known him for years.'

Claudia had come to a halt, glancing uncertainly at her husband for guidance. Her tall, thin spouse was calmly shaking hands with Leo. Angrily conscious that she might have made a fool of herself, Claudia gave Angie a filthy look. 'We'll discuss this matter in private.'

'If you don't mind, I'm going to bed now,' Angie replied with quiet dignity. 'Leo kept on ringing the bell. I had to let him in.'

She climbed the stairs, conscious that she had no hope of ultimately escaping one of Claudia's bossy lectures, but too weary and shaken by Leo's visit to care. Considering the length of Angie's employment with her, Claudia ought to be able to trust her by now not to invite an armed robber or child molester into the house. She was almost twenty-two, not a feckless teenage baby-sitter.

Yet Leo had made her feel very much like a teenager again, she conceded grudgingly—hot, bothered, awkward, over-sensitive to atmosphere. It had been embarrassment, she told herself—the embarrassment of memories that no woman with any pride would want to recall. And that was *all*.

Determined to be satisfied with that explanation, she climbed into the bed across the room from Jake's, having fought a very heavy battle against a feverish longing to snatch him out of bed and hug him tight to comfort herself. That would be selfish, and she was *not* a selfish mother...was she? No, of course she wasn't.

She put up with an employer who would have taxed the temper of a saint just so that Jake could eat well, live in a comfortable house and play in a spacious garden with lots of toys. So he had virtually nothing to call his own, and his clothes were all the twins' hand-me-downs, but he was still too little to appreciate those facts. This year she had wanted to give him a proper Christmas, though. That was why she had dared to risk Claudia's wrath to ask for more money, but the recollection of the earlier part of the evening could no longer hold her concentration...

It was almost impossible for her to believe that Wallace Neville was willing to entertain the butler's daughter at his vast ancestral home. Would he have invited her to stay in the main house, or would he have expected her to squash herself back into her father and stepmother's disgracefully damp and desolate little basement flat? And if Leo's grandfather *had* offered her financial help, would she have been weak enough to accept it?

Uneasy with the thought, Angie tossed and turned sleeplessly. It was out of the question anyway. Claudia would blow a gasket if Angie demanded time off over Christmas, and until Jake was old enough to start nursery school at least the Dicksons were their security.

Even so, she still lay awake, staring into the darkness, helplessly remembering the first time she had seen Leo when she was thirteen. Every Christmas and every summer he had come to stay with his grandfather, and although his English was perfect he had remained quintessentially Greek. Exotic, fascinating and extravagantly handsome, he had become the natural focus of Angie's first crush. Of course, eight years her senior, he had barely noticed that she was alive in those days.

During the summer when she was fourteen, Leo had brought a girlfriend with him. She had had a very irritating giggle. With intense amusement, Angie had watched Leo wince. But the following year laughter had been thin on the ground. Petrina Phillipides had come to visit—a porcelain-perfect and dainty little Greek heiress with a cloud of silky black hair and an elderly maiden aunt in tow as a chaperon. Angie had ground her teeth in disbelief while she had watched Leo fall in love. Couldn't he see that Petrina was too spoilt, too conceited, too empty-headed, with her silly clothes and even sillier hairstyles, to provide lasting appeal for an intelligent man?

No, Leo had been blind, and the summer after that Petrina had had even better reason to look smug. She had been wearing Leo's engagement ring. Angie had been aghast, but even then she hadn't given up all hope. After all, many an engagement was broken before the altar was reached, she had reasoned, snatching at straws.

However, when Wallace had finally flown out to Leo's wedding and no last-minute miracle had prevented the dreadful deed from being done, Angie had been inconsolable. But by then she had been seventeen, and thoroughly fed up with herself for ever having wasted time languishing over a male who had always been out of reach and who was now another woman's husband. So she had started dating herself and, boy, had she dated! Her five-foot-ten-inch model-slim body, symmetrical features and waist-length mane of pale blonde hair had ensured that she was never short of eager admirers.

Petrina had been sullenly pregnant that Christmas, and the unimpressed mother of a beautiful baby girl a few months later. Leo had adored his daughter. Angie's heart had ached when she'd seen him lavish unashamed love and warmth on little Jenny, who had been named after his late mother. Petrina had been an indifferent and petulant parent, thrusting her baby back at the nanny as soon as she decently could, visibly resenting the fact that her daughter and not herself was now the centre of attention. And Angie had thought, Oh, Leo, Leo…why didn't you wait for me to grow up?

But that very same year tragedy had intervened to destroy Leo's family. Christmas hadn't been celebrated at Deveraux Court. Wallace hadn't had the heart for it, and Leo had remained in Greece. His wife and his baby daughter had been killed in a car crash. That next summer, however, Leo had come back, alone and brooding, and he had taken up residence in the Folly by the lake, shunning all company.

And Angie, in her complete and utter stupidity, had decided that she was finally to have her chance with Leo, and that it had to be then or never, before he flew back to Greece and fell madly in love with some other unsuitable woman…

'Now that I know *who* Leo Demetrios is,' Claudia droned on in her most gracious mood the following afternoon, 'I realise that you could scarcely keep a man of his importance outside the house. But he has to be the single exception to the rule, Angie. Don't open that door again when we're out.'

Money fairly talked, Angie conceded grimly. Claudia had already been on the phone to all her friends, saying things in her carrying voice like, 'You'll never guess who we had in our house last night...the most *utterly* charming man... Must be worth *billions*... Yes, employs our au pair's father... Can you believe, she didn't even offer him a cup of coffee? Probably quite overpowered by him just turning up like that... I don't think Greeks can be as class-conscious as we are...'

Oh, don't you believe it, Angie reflected with gritted teeth as she slammed shut the door on the washing machine and switched it on to drown out Claudia's verbal ecstasy. When Leo had sobered up to a dawn that woke him to the unlovely reality that he was actually sharing a bed with the butler's daughter, he had vacated that bed so fast, Angie had been cut to the bone. But even then she had been poorly prepared for the blunt and wounding force of the rejection which had so swiftly concluded their brief intimacy and left her bereft of any hope...or pride.

The doorbell went. Angie padded through to the hall and then stopped dead in the porch. Through the side window, she could see the long, impressive bonnet of a chauffeur-driven limousine. Suddenly breathless with an undeniable sense of anticipation, she pulled open the door. Leo, a breathtakingly elegant vision in a dove-grey suit, white silk shirt and pale blue tie, gazed down at her. He looked drop-dead gorgeous.

And Angie's treacherous heartbeat hit a dizzy peak, as if she were riding a big dipper. The most intense and shattering surge of physical awareness paralysed her to the spot.

'I wasn't expecting you to come back,' Angie whispered.

Leo dealt her the most fleeting glance before flashing a

brilliant smile at something or someone over her shoulder. 'Mrs Dickson?'

'Claudia, *please*...' the brunette carolled.

Leo strode past Angie as if she were the invisible woman and grasped Claudia's eagerly extended hand.

'Leo...?' Angie muttered in confusion.

'I'm here to speak to your employer, Angie, if you would excuse us?'

'Come into the drawing room.' Claudia gave Leo a delighted smile. 'Make some coffee, Angie.'

Fizzing with incredulous annoyance at the dismissal, Angie went to put on the kettle then returned to the hall.

'*So* dreadfully sorry, but I'm afraid we couldn't possibly spare her at present. We'll have visitors staying over Christmas,' Claudia was saying apologetically.

Angie pressed the door wider and stood on the threshold, furious that she had been deliberately excluded from a discussion that related to her. How dared Leo do this? How dared he go over her head as if she were a child who could not speak up for herself?

'When *did* Angie last have a holiday?' Leo drawled softly from his stance by the marble fireplace.

Caught unprepared by the question, Claudia frowned. 'Well, er...'

'In fact, Angie doesn't receive holidays in this household, does she, Mrs Dickson?' Raw contempt glittered in Leo's steady gaze.

'Where on earth did you get that idea?' Claudia asked rather shrilly.

'Leo—' Angie began weakly.

'Angie's working conditions are the talk of the neighbourhood,' Leo countered with biting censure, his strong, hard-boned features grim. 'Indeed, sweatshop labour would be a generous description of her terms of employment within your home.'

'I...I beg your pardon?' Her face mottling with ugly colour, Claudia was openly shocked by the sudden attack.

'*Leo*, for heaven's sake!' Angie intervened in horror.

But Leo didn't even glance in her direction. 'You took advantage of a pregnant teenager. For more than two years you have worked her round the clock and paid her peanuts for the privilege. One has a duty of care towards one's staff, but you have disregarded that fact. As you are neither poor nor unintelligent, there is no extenuating circumstance which might excuse such unscrupulous behaviour.'

'How *dare* you speak to me like that? Get out of my house!' Claudia was now brick red with disbelieving fury.

'Go and pack, Angie,' Leo murmured without batting a magnificent eyelash; indeed, the curious beginnings of a smile were already tugging at the corners of his sensual mouth. 'I will wait in the car.'

'I'm not going anywhere...' Angie began unevenly.

'The *talk* of the neighbourhood, am I?' Claudia sent the younger woman a look of outraged accusation. 'When I think of what we've done for you—'

'You've done nothing but use her for your own selfish purposes,' Leo interposed with sardonic cool.

'You're sacked... I want you and that child of yours out of this house—*right now*!' Claudia screeched at Angie, full blast.

CHAPTER TWO

WHITE-FACED, Angie lugged a battered suitcase out through the front door with Claudia still shouting recriminations in her wake. A sturdy older man in a chauffeur's uniform was waiting in silent readiness to take her case. The front door slammed thunderously shut behind her.

Lifting an unsteady hand to press it to her pounding, perspiring brow, Angie hurried round the side of the house to the fenced-in back garden where Jake had mercifully remained throughout the agonising minutes it had taken for her to strip their room of their possessions. And with Claudia standing over her, bent on retribution, their possessions, such as they were, had shrunk alarmingly. The brunette had angrily refused to allow Angie to pack any of Jake's clothes, saying that the twins' cast-offs had only been given to her on loan and not to keep. She had maintained the same line when it came to Jake's toys, which the Dickson children had long since outgrown.

A frightening vision of her former employer forcibly stripping Jake to the buff in the teeth of the winter wind impelling her, Angie raced across the back garden to the sandpit and literally snatched Jake's sturdy little body into her arms. He looked up at her with a startled frown, huge dark eyes wide. 'Oh, Jake,' she almost sobbed as she cuddled her son close and buried her face momentarily in his sweet-smelling, springy black curls. 'I will kill Leo for doing this to you…I swear it!'

The chauffeur whipped open the passenger door of the limousine. Seeing that Claudia had now emerged from the house, Angie leapt in before Jake could be wrenched out of his shabby duffel coat and dungarees, not to mention his wellington boots.

As the chauffeur closed the door and walked round the bonnet at a stately pace which seemed to challenge Claudia's aggressive stance, the silence in the spacious, leather-upholstered back seat seemed to thunder. Struggling for breath, her breasts still heaving from her frantic rush to protect Jake from a direct collision with Claudia's malice, Angie glanced up. A stark frown drawing his winged black brows together, Leo was staring fixedly at the child on her lap.

'He is very…dark,' Leo selected after some hesitation.

Angie cloaked startled eyes and bent her head as she swung Jake off her knees onto the seat and began to fiddle with the belt to strap him safely in.

'I thought the child would be blond…' Leo added half under his breath, still staring as Jake swivelled to look up at him with lustrous dark brown eyes fringed with curling black lashes, the natural olive tone of his skin obvious against the white polo neck rolled under his dimpled chin.

In panic, Angie thought fast. 'He takes after my mother…she was as dark as a Celt. It happens that way sometimes—genes, you know, throwback genes,' Angie muttered rather wildly, and then, reddening, she compressed her lips.

'I never met your mother.'

Angie had been very much hoping that he hadn't for her late mother had been as blonde as her daughter. But her mother had only lived at Deveraux Court for a few months before she had walked out on her marriage, pregnant but preferring to go it alone rather than stay with a husband whom she had swiftly learned to despise for his lack of ambition.

Angie breathed in slowly and deeply. It didn't help to steady her leaping nerves or to subdue the dangerous surge of anger ready to explode from her lips. She focused on

Jake's down-bent dark head and faithfully promised herself that she would not raise her voice and risk upsetting her son.

'Do you realise what you've done?' Her low-pitched enquiry shook with the effort it took to control her temper.

'*Theos*... It is beginning to sink in,' Leo confessed with outrageous calm. 'I cannot take you to Deveraux Court until Thursday at the earliest. Wallace has guests. It would be inappropriate for you to arrive while they remain.'

Angie trembled and threw her head up, eyes shimmering like piercing blue arrows of accusation. 'You have deprived my son of the only home and security he has ever known...'

'You should be thanking me.' Bold black eyes instantly challenged her.

'Th-thanking you?' Angie stammered in disbelief.

'How could you remain in that house enslaved by that harpy? Where is your spirit and sense, that you should've accepted such terms for so long?'

As raw rage splintered explosively through Angie's slender frame, she sucked in oxygen like a drowning swimmer in an effort to contain it. 'I stayed for my son's benefit,' she bit out tautly. 'I was able to be with him all day...and he's enjoyed many advantages there that I could never have given him.'

'I made a polite approach and a most modest request. That woman was not reasonable,' Leo asserted, smoothly disclaiming all responsibility.

'You interfered in something which was none of your business, and you gave Claudia precisely two minutes to snap to attention and do your bidding before you went on the offensive. I told you there was no way that I could leave the Dicksons over Christmas... I *told* you that nothing on earth would persuade me to go back to Deveraux Court,' Angie reminded him in a steadily rising crescendo. 'But you wouldn't listen, and now we're homeless and I'm out of a job!'

Leo cast her a gleaming look of reproof. 'Drop the dramatics, Angie. Naturally, I will assume responsibility for you both until such time as Wallace relieves me of the necessity.'

Angie was so close to exploding, she couldn't trust herself to speak.

'Thursday, you go to Deveraux Court and eat humble pie. I don't care if it chokes you. It is the price of reacceptance, and you will pay it,' Leo informed her with daunting conviction. 'Today I did you a favour.'

Angie gulped. 'A favour? As of this moment, my son has only the clothes he is wearing and not one single toy to his name—'

'Waff.' Jake spoke up for the first time, with an air of expectancy. 'Want Waff...'

Angie froze in dismay. 'Waff's at home, darling,' she muttered weakly. 'He couldn't come.'

Jake scowled, looking so shockingly like a miniature version of his father that for an instant Angie could not believe that Leo had not guessed the truth the minute he'd seen him. 'Want Waff...Waff like cars too.'

Angie swallowed the great lump threatening her throat and shot Leo a look of accusing censure. 'Perhaps you would like to explain that the T-O-Y,' she spelt out, 'which he has slept with every night of his life, no longer belongs to him.'

'What are you talking about? Ah...you mean you were careless enough to forget it in your rushed departure.'

'N-no, that's not what I meant,' Angie managed unevenly. 'All his clothes and almost all his playthings originally belonged to Claudia's children and she refused to let me remove any of them from the house—not very surprising, after the way you insulted her. She couldn't get back at you, so she took her temper out on my child instead!'

His lean, dark features stiffened with incredulous comprehension. 'His clothes...his *toys*?'

Angie nodded jerkily.

'Toy,' Jake said doggedly. 'Waff toy.'

'So we buy some more—particularly this Waff thing,' Leo gritted with stark impatience. 'I wouldn't have believed that any woman could exercise such petty spite!'

'A W-A-F-F cannot be bought at any price,' Angie informed him in a voice thick with condemnation and a deep inner dread of Jake's bedtime. 'It was made by Claudia's grandmother for Sophia. It's a pink giraffe.'

Leo spread unimpressed and autocratic lean brown hands. 'I will buy a proper giraffe.'

'It won't fool him, Leo.' Slowly, numbly, Angie shook her aching head, wondering why she was focusing on a humble but much loved soft toy when she didn't even know where they would be sleeping tonight. 'Where are you planning to take us?'

'My town house—where else?'

'I'm not going home with you!' Angie exclaimed in shock.

'Home,' Jake said more cheerfully. 'Waff...'

'He's obsessed,' Leo remarked disapprovingly.

'He's still only a baby,' Angie said defensively. 'How could you do this to us?'

'With the greatest of ease. I did what was right—'

'*Right?*'

'For better or for worse your child is a Neville. He is a part of my family circle,' Leo ground out in grudging concession. 'He should not suffer for the faults of his parents.'

Angie slung him a scorching glance. 'I am not at fault as a parent in any way.'

'I would suggest that we save this conversation until we are alone.'

'I don't want to go to your house,' Angie told him between clenched teeth.

'I'm not checking you into a hotel. You might be stupid enough to disappear again, and I have wasted enough time tracking you down—'

'I thought it was Wallace who—'

'My grandfather is in his eighties,' Leo reminded her drily. 'I employed the investigation agency and dealt with them, and you were far from easily found.'

'I didn't want to be found,' Angie whispered in sudden, dragging weariness, her taut shoulders slumping in defeat.

Silence fell. For a minute or two, she stared blindly out at the passing traffic but then slowly she turned until she was watching Leo instead. The relaxation of his impressive lean length had an indolent quality which mocked her own explosive tension, yet was, in its own way, highly deceptive for there was nothing indolent about Leo. A white-hot core of raw energy drove him, not to mention his fierce Greek pride. And even without that spectacular bone structure and build Leo would have commanded attention in any company for he had a presence equalled by few men, and women were mesmerised by the high-voltage charge of his intense sexuality.

His hard, classic profile turned, brilliant dark eyes catching her out, lingering unashamedly as she coloured, his lush lashes dropping low to study her intently with nothing of her own inhibition. A curl of heat clenched her stomach and tensed every muscle in her slender body.

'I was afraid that you might have ended up on the streets.' Leo broke the silence with that devastatingly candid admission.

Her jaw dropping, Angie's eyes widened in outrage.

'It was a natural fear,' Leo stated quietly. 'What money you had wouldn't have lasted long in a city like this. I believed that you might be forced to rely on your looks to survive.'

'No. I wasn't quite that desperate.' Angie's hands closed

fiercely together on her lap, her voice shaky but acidic. 'I got by—*without* relying on my looks.'

'And I can only hope that the experience taught you a lesson. Drew was dazzled by you, but he always planned to marry money. Only a wealthy woman could afford to keep my cousin in the style he believes to be his due,' Leo delivered with supreme scorn.

'I don't want to talk about Drew.' Hatred was burning like a bright, blinding light inside Angie's battered heart at that moment. 'Right now, I'm just trying to come to terms with what you have done to our lives.'

Leo smiled slightly, very much as a lion might have smiled at a puny and not very bright prey. 'Soon you will be grateful for my interference.'

'Never. You can't play with people's lives like this!' But even as Angie told him that she felt as if she was spouting hot air.

Penniless, homeless, jobless. Leo had destroyed everything they had. And Leo had done the unforgivable—he had put her in the degrading position of having to accept that they were now dependent on *his* generosity. That devastated her pride and stuck in her throat like an indigestible concrete block, but, with a small child's needs to consider, she couldn't just walk away in a temper...for where would she walk *to*?

The car drew up outside a large, impressive town house in a quiet, elegant square. Angie climbed out and reached for Jake, but he scrambled out on his own, deliberately evading her hand, displaying the wilful and stubborn independent streak which she was seeing more and more as he left babyhood behind. An older woman had the front door open even before they reached the top step. She bent her greying head, her attention locking onto Jake and staying there.

'My housekeeper, Epifania. She will see to the child,' Leo informed Angie.

'The child'. Angie swore that she would scream if Leo used that phrase just one more time within her hearing. '*I* will see to him.'

'Epifania was once my nursemaid,' Leo revealed drily. 'I can assure you that she is more than capable of managing one small boy.'

Epifania dragged her attention from Jake, glanced fleetingly at Angie and then swiftly away again to attend to her employer's instructions.

Leo's nursemaid. This definitely wasn't her day, Angie conceded, turning pink with discomfiture. The Greek woman might well notice the resemblance, particularly if she had looked after Leo when he'd been the same age. But how likely was it that the housekeeper would risk causing offence by making any comment? Angie told herself that her secret was safe.

After all, she had no intention of telling Leo that he was the father of her son. Why? It would mean exposing her own lie and taking advantage of Leo in a way that even now she could not bear to do. It wouldn't be fair because she had quite deliberately run the risk of becoming pregnant. Indeed, hard as it was to recall without a shamed feeling of self-loathing, Angie had actually *wanted* to conceive that weekend.

More than anything else, she had longed to give Leo a child to replace the one he had lost. And she simply hadn't thought beyond that crazy, spur-of-the-moment decision...or had she? At the back of her mind, hadn't she also believed that Leo might find it almost impossible to walk away from the mother of his child? Inwardly, Angie shrank from the depth of calculation which Leo would read into her past behaviour if she admitted that Jake was his son.

She had been stupid and reckless, had known the instant that Leo rejected her just *how* stupid. She had been hopelessly in love with him and very immature. But Leo would neither understand nor forgive what she had done. He would assume that she had lied to ensnare him because he was a very rich man. With a confession of theft hanging over her head, what else could he possibly think? He would scarcely attribute any purer motive to her planned pregnancy.

Concluding his conversation with Epifania, who already had Jake in her arms, Leo cast open a door. 'We can talk now, Angie,' he murmured, yet the soft assurance somehow fell on her ears with all the weight of a threat.

Scolding herself for that fancy, she preceded him into a wonderfully furnished library and, glimpsing her own reflection in the gilded mirror on the wall opposite, she winced. Her hair was in a wild, wind-blown tangle, her face bare of make-up because cosmetics were among the many things she had quickly learned weren't a necessity. She was wearing a black sweater, jeans and a fleece jacket, all of which had been bought second-hand from charity shops.

She looked poor and shabby, and she was standing in a room decorated with a truly awesome disregard for expense, with its discreetly gleaming antique furniture, ornate floor-length curtains, fresh flowers and glowing Persian rugs. Digging her hands into her pockets, she glanced uneasily at Leo.

Lounging back against the edge of a mahogany desk in a stray patch of sunlight, he was watching her, brilliant, beautiful eyes now boldly and ruthlessly appraising. Caught unprepared, Angie felt that appraisal like a physical touch. Her slender figure tensed, colour staining her taut cheekbones as she found herself inexorably meeting that look. And just as suddenly she was running out of breath, mouth drying, heartbeat racing as she connected with the electrifying shimmer of those dark golden eyes. Heat like an insidious spark that built terrifyingly fast into a forest fire blazed deep in the pit of her stomach.

Slowly Leo uncoiled himself, straightened and strolled, sure-footed and silent as a prowling predator, towards her.

Her throat closed over convulsively, her lips parting as she strove with every atom of her being to break away from the compelling stare. He halted two feet away from her and the silence between them stretched tighter and tighter until it clawed at her nerves.

'Alone at last,' Leo purred with intense satisfaction.

Angie blinked in bemusement. Her heart was pounding so frighteningly fast, she was convinced it might burst.

'Tell me,' Leo continued in that same mesmeric undertone that sent a shiver of the most appalling sexual awareness down her rigid spinal cord.

'Tell you what?' Something like pure panic beginning to assail her as she registered how she was reacting to his proximity, Angie stepped back from him.

Leo merely closed the distance again, virtually cornering her against the bookshelves. 'I ask only for an honest answer to one very simple question. It is a question which I have had to wait a very long time to ask. Did you use me like man bait to make Drew jealous? *Or*...did you end up in bed with him on the rebound from me?'

As Leo calmly resurrected the past—or *his* version of the past—sheer shock immobilised Angie. The tip of her tongue flicked out nervously to moisten her full lower lip. Leo's gaze narrowed and dropped to follow the tiny movement, his entire attention nailed to the generous pink curve of her mouth.

Momentarily released from his forceful scrutiny, Angie sucked in an audible, sharp, swift breath of relief and gasped, 'Neither!'

'Oh, it has to be one of them—unless you have the morals of a whore, and I would be most reluctant to assume that of a girl of nineteen,' Leo informed her with ruthless cynicism. 'I'm giving you the benefit of the doubt in conceding that perhaps you felt something for *one* of us!'

Angie flinched and turned scarlet simultaneously, anger flaring in her bright blue eyes. 'You have no right to ask.'

'Two men…and one very, very beautiful girl,' Leo spelt out slowly. 'A recipe for disaster when the very beautiful girl was also impulsive, passionate and rebellious.'

'I don't know why you're talking to me like this. I don't like it.'

Unmoved dark eyes rested on her. 'That won't make me stop asking because I need to know. Drew always wanted you…but he never wanted you more than when he thought you were mine.'

Angie jerked her blonde head away, her stomach muscles clenching in dismay at his persistence and his insight. He wasn't telling her anything she hadn't known but, ironically, she had never been attracted to Drew. Compared to Leo, he had been like gilt beside gold, always overshadowed and diminished. But, for all that, Drew's attention had been balm to her savaged ego after Leo had ditched her.

And for a while she had gone around with Drew and his friends, nightclubbing and partying, deaf to her father's outraged disapproval. Was that how the belief that her child was Drew's had come about? she wondered abstractedly. Or had she been so incoherent in her distress the day that Wallace found her with the miniature portrait that she had left the old man suffering from a genuine misapprehension?

Lean brown fingers reached out and tugged a long strand of silvery pale hair. 'Angie…?'

Her eyes flew back to Leo, and he was so close that her nostrils flared on the warm and achingly familiar scent of him. A long shiver racked her and her eyes collided unwarily with his darkly intent gaze. A hint of cruel amusement gleamed in his eyes.

'Stop it,' she whispered jerkily.

'Stop what? Playing games?' An unrepentant winged ebony brow climbed. 'Why? You played plenty with me that summer.'

The colour drained from Angie's cheeks, leaving her
pale.

'*Theos*...of course, I knew,' Leo drawled very drily.
'Like Artemis, goddess of the chase and the forest, you
hunted me down. It would've taken a stronger male than I
to withstand the temptation you offered.'

Angie wanted to sink through the floor. Unable to ex-
ecute that feat, she sidled along the shelving instead, desperate to escape. 'I'd better go and check on Jake.'

Long tanned fingers closed round her wrist and tugged
her inexorably back within reach. 'Not so fast,' Leo murmured with deceptive gentleness. 'You haven't answered
my question yet.'

Angie had the demeaning suspicion that she was playing
mouse to Leo's cat. Abruptly, her chin came up, denying
that image. 'There's one possibility that doesn't seem to
have occurred to you...'

'And what is that?'

'Maybe, at the end of the day, I couldn't tell the difference between you and Drew,' Angie clarified with a studied
desire to insult.

In reward, a dark rush of blood fired over Leo's blunt
cheekbones, his savagely handsome features suddenly
wiped clean of every ounce of mockery. His lean face hardening, he leant forward without warning and planted two
spread hands on the shelves on either side of her head,
effectively imprisoning her with the solid breadth and
strength of his supremely powerful physique.

'*Ohi*...no?' Leo questioned with a shockingly intimidating blaze of anger in his glittering stare.

Angie's spine grated into bruising collision with the
shelving as she instinctively attempted to back away from
that dangerous fire. 'Leo...'

Long fingers whipped across to curve on her cheekbones
and hold her still. 'Let me teach you the difference,' Leo
gritted darkly.

'No—'

But as her anxious gaze melded with the drowning darkness of his explosive anticipation tore through her like a storm warning, tightening every muscle and firing every nerve-ending with tortured expectancy. With a guttural sound somewhere between a harsh laugh and a groan, Leo dropped his strong hands to the swell of her hips and took her mouth hotly and hungrily with his own.

He crushed her to him, and the very blood in her veins sang with the heat of her excitement. Under the onslaught of his demanding lips and the carnal thrust of his tongue, Angie burned. He ravaged her mouth with the fierce heat of an innately sexual male, hell-bent on possession, and she fell victim to a hot and disorientating tide of intimate memory that tore down every remaining barrier and reduced her to submissive rubble.

As suddenly as he had reached for her, Leo dragged his mouth from hers again. Glittering dark eyes cloaked, he thrust himself back from her and strode over to the window.

For a split second, Angie thought she might slide down to the rug because her knees were ready to fold beneath her. For a split second, Angie didn't even recall where she was. But her body ached and pulsed in a way she had almost forgotten, sensually alive and hurting in a way she did not want to acknowledge. She felt the swollen tenderness of her breasts, the painful sense of tormenting emptiness between her thighs, and shivered in disbelieving horror that Leo could still have that devastating an effect on her body.

She studied his back view with stricken eyes, reading the savage tension in his broad shoulders and the rigid bracing of his long, powerful thighs. And just as swiftly she suspected that that sudden flare of physical hunger and even more physical connection might have been no more welcome to him.

'The difference between my cousin and I,' Leo framed

rawly as he swung back to face her, burnished, censorious dark eyes like flaring arrows of gold, 'is that I was ashamed of what happened between us two and a half years ago!'

'Ashamed?' Angie repeated sickly.

'*Cristos*…what else?' Leo demanded in a wrathful growl of rebuke. 'What did you expect? My wife had been dead only seven months…and you were nineteen and naive as they come, for all your wiles! Did you think I could be proud of making such a conquest? The teenage daughter of one of my grandfather's most loyal and trusted dependants? And, even worse, a virgin?'

CHAPTER THREE

ANGIE had turned to stone, the pallor of her perfect features pronounced but rigidly uninformative—for one necessary skill she had learned working for Claudia was the ability to keep her face devoid of expression. But, inside herself, she was cringing. 'Conquest'...'dependant'...'virgin'...Not one single term welcome to her ears—indeed each and every one of them emphasising the humiliating inequality which had always divided her from Leo.

In bitter mortification, she flew out of the room and down the hall, not even knowing where she was going in an unfamiliar house. Espying a cloakroom, she hurriedly and gratefully took refuge there. No, she had never had the advantage of a level playing field with Leo, she conceded wretchedly. Everything had separated them—age, background and experience. But, worst of all, she had met Leo in the time-warp world of Deveraux Court, leaving herself forever fixed in his mind as the butler's daughter and never, it seemed, to be anything else.

Why on earth had he kissed her? The ultimate put-down? Her insult had drawn an overwhelmingly primitive masculine response. But then, in the grip of strong emotion, Leo was no English gentleman of restraint, and he was very highly sexed. A dangerous little quiver of remembrance ran through Angie and her face burned with shame. She had no excuse to offer for her own behaviour. Leo still attracted her in much the same way that a magnet attracted iron filings. But it was just a physical thing now, she told herself with driven defensiveness—all down to body chemistry and hormones, and nothing whatsoever to do with her emotions.

A knock sounded on the door. Angie ignored it.

'Angie, you have a count of five to show yourself...'

Leo's warning sent Angie flying for a towel to dry her face with, which she had splashed thoroughly with cold water in the forlorn hope of cooling herself down.

She unlocked the door. 'Where's Jake?' she questioned stiffly, focusing on Leo's pale blue silk tie.

'Upstairs with Epifania. Listen,' Leo advised impatiently.

And she heard Jake's delighted chortles of glee filtering down from the floor above. Her son sounded as if he was having a whale of a time.

'I don't want to talk about the past!' Angie stated fiercely.

'It's unfinished business. I want it dealt with,' Leo countered without apology.

Angie flung her head high, blue eyes darkened by stress. 'There was nothing unfinished about it. You made yourself perfectly plain at the time—sorry, Angie, I needed a woman and I was drunk!' she interpreted with a raw bitterness she could not conceal.

Leo's even white teeth gritted. 'That *wasn't* what I said—'

'That's what it came down to!' In too much pain from her memories to find such proximity to Leo bearable, Angie wrapped her arms around herself in a starkly protective movement. 'Don't you ever touch me again. Once bitten, forever shy!'

Leo sent her a flashfire glance of involuntary amusement. 'That rejection routine of yours needs some extensive work and application.'

A deep flush of mortification lit Angie's cheeks as he reminded her of her eager response in his arms. Her skin felt super-thin, as if the tiniest dent might wound her to the death. And it was Leo who was doing that to her, and that appalled her because she had honestly believed that Leo could not have the power to hurt her any more. She had buried that foolish teenager deep and fancied herself mature beyond imagining. Now she was discovering her error.

Leo curved a hand over her tense shoulder and she flinched away. He vented a soft, soothing sound that was terrifyingly sexy. 'You're trembling...'

'I'll never forgive you for bringing me here! Where the heck are we supposed to go now? I'm not crawling back to Deveraux Court to grovel—*or* eat humble pie—so where does that leave us?'

Leo surveyed her mutinous face with reflective cool. 'Enjoying my hospitality,' he supplied smoothly, and swung on his heel.

'But I don't want to accept your hospitality, Leo.'

Leo stilled, and responded without turning his arrogant dark head. 'In five days' time, you will have seen sense and you will be heading to the Court. If you haven't the wit to grovel, you will undoubtedly feel the rough edge of Wallace's tongue—but then that's your business, *not* mine.'

As he left her standing there, Angie felt horribly alone and scared for the first time in a long while. The feeling of insecurity gripping her now was intense. The very last place she wanted to go was Deveraux Court, and the very last place she wanted to stay was in Leo's house.

She finally headed upstairs, where the housekeeper showed her into a large bedroom which connected with the even more spacious room where the older woman had been keeping Jake occupied. An evening meal was suggested, and her son's likes and dislikes were discussed in almost embarrassing detail.

But not by word, look or gesture did Epifania even hint that Jake might be anything more than the child of a guest. Angie scolded herself for the guilty conscience which had made her far too imaginative earlier. Of course Epifania hadn't spotted any instant resemblance which linked Jake to her employer! Clearly the housekeeper was just extremely fond of children.

Forty minutes later, Angie and her son were summoned down to eat. One solitary place was set at the massive polished table in the imposing gold and blue dining room, and, to the left of it, a high chair for Jake. Evidently Leo was not to join them. But then undoubtedly Leo did not dine at so early an hour. When Angie took Jake back upstairs, a positive feast of plush soft toys and a small mound of packages awaited them in his bedroom. A giant furry giraffe was prominent in the spread.

As Jake whooped in delight and rushed to investigate, Angie stilled in surprise and dismay on the threshold.

'You see? A young child is easily distracted with new toys,' Leo drawled with cool superiority from behind her.

Sharply disconcerted because she hadn't heard his approach, Angie whipped round. 'Where did all these things come from?'

'A friend made the selection for me and had them sent over. There should be some clothes as well.'

Angie reddened with discomfiture. 'And how much did this generous gesture of yours cost?'

Leo shifted a relaxed shoulder in a dismissive shrug. 'That's irrelevant.'

'Is it?' Angie queried with embarrassed heat. 'Surely you can appreciate that I can't accept this stuff?'

'It was nothing…forget it,' Leo responded drily.

'But I can't let you just pay for it all!'

His beautifully expressive mouth curled. 'Don't make me drag up that past you're so very reluctant to recall.'

'And what's that supposed to mean?'

'When it comes to moral principles, we both know you are not Pollyanna.'

Understanding came too late to protect Angie from that humiliating reminder. She turned white as if Leo had struck her. He was referring to the thefts.

Leo made an impatient movement with one brown hand. 'Try just to be yourself around me, Angie. I loathe hypoc-

risy…and all this fuss about a few necessities for a child?
Who do you think you are impressing with this charade of
objections?'

Angie backed unsteadily into the bedroom and closed the
door. She wanted to race back out again and grab Leo by
his arrogant, judgemental throat and scream, I am not a
thief! She wanted to proclaim her innocence with the very
strongest force. But she had surrendered that right of her
own volition over two years ago. Only by naming the true
culprit could she clear her own name, and, if she did that,
she would *still* cause unthinkable damage…

Leo would not allow even a reformed and deeply repen-
tant thief to remain in his grandfather's home. He would
bring in the police and press charges without hesitation.
Leo had no liberal convictions where crime and punishment
were concerned.

Lost in increasingly distressing introspection, Angie undressed Jake and bathed him in the *en suite*. Leo despised
her for her apparent greed and dishonesty. Why hadn't she
faced up to that harsh fact sooner? Just minutes ago, his
distaste and anger had rung out as clear as a bell. And she
had drawn his censure by daring to behave as if she wasn't
the greedy, grasping profiteer and eager free-loader he undoubtedly saw her as. Leo believed she had got off too
lightly for her sins. And no doubt he also thought that returning to Deveraux Court to grovel to Wallace and cringe
at the knowledge that everyone knew her to be a thief was
a long-overdue slice of her just desserts.

The packages revealed a sensible skeleton wardrobe for
Jake. Underwear and pyjamas, a duo of sweaters, shirts and
trousers, all bearing the brand name of a reasonably priced
chain store—unlike the array of blatantly expensive toys.
Sighing, Angie tucked Jake into the comfortable single bed.
Over-tired now, her son flipped fussily between the soft
toys which had earlier enthralled him, and then he said that
fatal word which Angie had been hoping not to hear.

'Waff...where Waff?'

'Waff's not here. I'm sorry,' Angie groaned as Jake's bottom lip began to wobble alarmingly, big dark eyes suddenly flooding with tears.

'Want Waff!' Jake sobbed.

Fifteen minutes of lamentations later, the housekeeper had joined Angie in her efforts to console and distract Jake, but the whole house continued to echo with the boy's noisy, convulsive sobs.

Without warning, Leo strode in. In an off-white dinner jacket and black silk bow-tie, he was clearly on his way out for the evening. He cast a grim glance down at Jake, an abandoned slump of utter misery on the bed. 'Your son knows how to get what he wants.'

'That's not fair, Leo,' Angie muttered in reproach.

Releasing his breath in a slow, driven hiss, Leo crouched fluidly down beside the bed and gently shook Jake's shoulder to gain his attention. 'Jake...I'm going to get Waff.'

'Don't make promises you can't keep,' Angie hissed, but it was too late. Her son's damp, tousled head had come off the pillow and a look of pathetic hope was already blossoming in his tear-drenched eyes.

'If George Dickson wants to be sued through the courts for a pink giraffe, I'll do it,' Leo swore, vaulting upright again.

'Don't be daft...that would take forever.'

'Give me an hour... George struck me as a very level-headed and rational man.'

Stunned, Angie watched him stride back out again. Leo was planning to drive over to the Dicksons' to demand custody of a pink giraffe? Jake sat up, rubbing at his eyes. 'Waff...?' he mumbled with a hint of a wobbly smile.

'Wait and see...maybe,' Angie said carefully.

Leo was back, however, within the hour. He came through the door with Waff extended like a small but tremendously important peace offering. Jake shot out of bed like a jet-propelled missile, hurled himself ecstatically at Leo's knees and accepted Waff back, tucking the battered toy possessively under his arm. 'Night, night,' he said happily, accepting Angie's help to climb back into bed.

'How did you do it?' Angie whispered as Leo moved back to the door again.

'Dickson was so embarrassed, he couldn't hand Waff over fast enough. He sends his apologies for what he termed "an unfortunate misunderstanding",' Leo informed Angie very drily over his shoulder.

'Really?' Angie followed Leo out into the corridor. 'What else did he say?'

'I'm afraid I don't have the time to tell you.'

Belatedly, Angie reread the significance of the dinner jacket he wore and flushed uncomfortably. 'You're running late again.'

His dark eyes gleamed as he studied her. 'And tomorrow morning I'm flying over to Brussels for a few days. You'll have the house to yourself until Thursday.'

He went on down the stairs, and Angie listened to the distant thud of the front door and glanced in at Jake again. Leo's son had gone out like a light, Waff a barely visible pink splodge tucked under his chin. For some reason she found that she couldn't stop wondering who the lady in Leo's life was... Did *she* play games? Probably not. Games were the province of the young and brash and insecure, she reminded herself heavily. And quite the reverse of appealing when recognised for what they were by the quarry.

In the early hours, Angie lay awake. Leo hadn't come home, Leo obviously wasn't *coming* home—and why had she been unconsciously straining to hear his return? she asked herself with angry self-loathing. Take the average single male on a Saturday night—he did not sit in toasting his feet by the fire. When that same male was also gorgeous, rich, oversexed and spoilt for female choice, he was undoubtedly involved in an intimate relationship, and extremely unlikely to come racing home like Cinderella, struggling to beat the clock at midnight.

Switching on the light, she peered at her alarm clock. Almost two. The house was silent as the grave. Desperate for something to read to pass the time, she slid out of bed, automatically reached for her towelling dressing gown and then realised that, in her eagerness to escape Claudia, she hadn't retrieved it, *or* several other garments which she could ill afford to lose, from the wash. More things to replace, and she had barely five pounds to her name, she reflected dully. Furthermore Christmas was hurtling towards them at breakneck speed and she had next to nothing bought for Jake.

She crept downstairs and into the library. Surprise, surprise... Leo's shelves were packed with books written in Greek. As she began flipping irritably through a pile of business magazines in search of something lighter, the door suddenly opened. In fright, Angie almost jumped a foot in the air.

Bold dark eyes whipped over her paralysed figure. 'What are you doing in here?'

Recovering, Angie pushed an awkward hand through her tumbled hair. 'I was looking for something to read—'

'On my desk?' Leo prompted drily, possibly because she was standing only a foot from it with the air of being caught in mid-flight.

'I haven't been anywhere near your desk,' Angie muttered defensively, backing away from it as Leo moved slowly forward. 'I was glancing through the magazines on that chair.'

'Since when were you interested in electronics?'

Angie stared at him. His black hair was tousled. His bow-tie was missing and his shirt partially unbuttoned, revealing a disturbing triangle of brown skin and the start of the riot of dark, curling hair that she knew covered his pectoral muscles. Embarrassed by that knowledge and the memory, Angie momentarily shut her eyes. But still she saw Leo standing there, strong jawline blue-shadowed with the same early-morning stubble which had once felt so interestingly, arousingly rough against her softer, smoother skin.

Inside her own head, she shrieked at her treacherous subconscious to leave her alone and stop throwing up things she didn't want to remember—most particularly when it was obvious that Leo had recently vacated some other woman's bed. As that conviction assailed her, a searing spasm of hot jealousy and resentment shot through Angie, leaving her deeply shaken.

'Were you looking for money?'

Her dazed and troubled eyes flew wide. 'M-money?' she stammered blankly.

Leo gave her a grim smile. 'Somehow I don't think you have graduated to safe-cracking yet.'

As Angie grasped his meaning, pain and anger combined in the bitter look she threw at him. 'Damn you to hell, Leo. I wouldn't *steal* from you!' she flung at him, and turned strickenly away, devastated by the extent of his distrust.

'You don't need to,' Leo breathed harshly. 'I'll give you money if you want it.'

Angie covered her anguished face with spread hands. 'You swine! I was only looking for something to read because I couldn't sleep!'

'I wish you had been a kleptomaniac,' Leo drawled softly. 'Intellectually, I could have dealt with kleptomania. But sadly the victims of that particular illness hoard what they take—they don't sell it on for profit…as you did.'

Snatching in a shuddering breath, Angie whirled back to him with clenched fists. 'I don't want to talk about it—'

'I'm afraid it left rather a bitter taste in my mouth when I worked out that, if you were the thief, you stole from my grandfather the very day before you shared my bed,' Leo admitted, his relentless dark eyes scanning her taut face.

'I *said* that I didn't want to talk about it!' Angie launched at him furiously.

'And you must have been remarkably nifty in that particular operation. As I recall you spent most of that morning riding so that you could accidentally on purpose keep on bumping into me on the estate. You then brought me lunch, which you had definitely made with your own fair hands because it was infinitely superior to anything Wallace's geriatric cook could possibly have prepared,' Leo continued with a disturbing glimmer of raw amusement breaking through the forbidding cast of his features.

'Leo…' Angie gritted.

'After lunch, you spent the afternoon haunting the woods round the lake and gathering flowers in a basket…most picturesque. My evening meal you also supplied and that same night you walked Wallace's dog until it almost dropped dead with exhaustion. In fact, your pursuit of me was very much a f-full-time occupation…'

As Leo's increasingly unsteady voice broke down altogether, his hard dark face suddenly slashed into a breathtakingly charismatic smile, and he threw his arrogant head back and laughed with uninhibited appreciation. '*Cristos*… Angie, when I watched you struggling to carry that fat old dog home, I was doubled up!'

Angie had stood there listening to that recitation of her past behaviour with an initially defiant and unmoved stare, but, as Leo had persisted in enumerating the lengths her desperate desire to be noticed by him had driven her to, boiling mortification had engulfed her in waves of regret. 'I'm so glad I entertained you!' she snapped, and tried to sidestep him.

Leo reached out and stilled her in her tracks with strong hands, laughter dying out of his strikingly handsome features to leave only a flaring, drugging intensity in his bold black eyes. 'You made me laugh…and, at the time, I was very grateful.'

'Let go of me—'

'I was intending to ask where you found the time that day to flex light fingers, but right now I don't really care,' Leo confided, his rich, dark drawl thickening and deepening on that startling admission. 'Not when I have you in my arms half-naked…'

Angie's eyes widened, and dropped in belated awareness to the green nightshirt she wore. There was nothing remotely provocative about its crew neckline or the hem that came to her knees. Even deeper colour staining her cheeks, she gazed up at him in angry reproach. 'I am *not* half-naked.'

Leo was not listening. 'The average Greek male does not require even this much encouragement when he is presented with a beautiful blonde, *pethi mou*,' he informed her in an earthy amused undertone as he banded his arms slowly round her.

'What are you d-doing?' Angie gasped, heart hammering in shock as he determinedly brought her into contact with his tautly muscular length and the heat of his big, powerful body penetrated the fine cotton she wore, suddenly making her feel as if she was indeed only semi-clothed. 'Leo…'

Burning dark eyes gazed down into hers. 'You quiver when I touch you…and you can scarcely be impervious to the effect you're having on me.'

Angie was trembling, face flushing hot pink as Leo shamelessly clamped his hands to the curve of her hips and hauled her into collision with the unmistakable thrust of his hard male arousal. Her legs went hollow, her nipples pinching into agonisingly erect peaks as a wave of the most terrifying and shameless yearning swept over her, and she fought it with all her might. 'Don't be disgusting.'

Leo dropped his head lower, his breath softly fanning her temples, shimmering dark golden eyes holding her in shivering stasis. 'If I can surrender to my desire, so can you...'

'No!'

'I see that same hunger in you, *feel* it,' Leo delivered with husky satisfaction. 'I saw it last night, swore I would play hard to get for at least a few days... But what a waste of time and opportunity that would be. Let's go to bed.'

That word, 'bed,' beckoned like a sensual invitation to paradise, and Angie hated herself so much for her own weakness of both body and will-power that that self-loathing gave her the strength to tear herself free of Leo's powerfully seductive spell.

'If I went to bed with you again, I'd deserve to be hung, drawn and quartered!' Angie slung at him wildly as she pulled back from him. 'And I can't imagine why you think I still want you like that...because I don't; I really don't!'

'*Cristos*... Of course you do!' Leo shot back at her with a look of impatience. 'Why do you think I ensured you would be with me by tonight?'

Barely able to assemble her thoughts, Angie nonetheless caught the truly shattering drift of that blunt admission. 'Ensured?' she queried. 'How could you possibly have *ensured* that I would be here?'

Leo's mouth twisted. 'Your former employer leapt at the provocation I offered and reacted exactly as I had foreseen.'

Angie was so taken aback by that confession, she just gaped at him.

'Angie, I had no intention of leaving that house without you. Why do you think I brought the limo?' he asked drily. 'Only a complete idiot would try to transport a woman, a child and all their worldly possessions in a Ferrari!'

'You got me thrown out of that house *deliberately*...' Angie was horrified by his complete lack of scruples and the even greater arrogance which had prompted him to freely admit it. She studied him with appalled blue eyes.

'Dear heaven...how could you be so selfish and destructive?'

'I acted in your best interests,' Leo countered.

Abruptly, Angie backed away from him, utterly chilled by that dispassionate response. 'It was an absolutely unforgivable thing to do to us—you don't even *understand* that, do you?' she condemned shakily. 'But then how could someone like you understand what it feels like to be broke, unemployed and without a roof over your head when you have a child's needs to consider?'

Leo dealt her a smouldering look. 'Whatever happens with Wallace, I will personally ensure that your circumstances will be vastly improved from what they were in that house. That is a promise.'

Her teeth clenched, eyes wild with censure. 'Oh, that's so big of you, Leo! But your help would come at a cost, wouldn't it? Something for nothing not being a goal you're famed for following!'

'What the hell is that supposed to mean?' Leo growled.

'And you were *so* patronising and superior just a few short hours ago!' Angie recalled with fierce mortification. 'What was that about me needing to learn the lesson that I couldn't rely on my looks to survive? And exactly what are *you* offering me, Leo?'

Slow-building anger now glittered in Leo's shimmering dark eyes. 'I am only offering you what we both know you want.'

Angie flinched. 'A sleazy roll in the hay with an oversexed louse who has just climbed out of some other woman's bed?' she bit out painfully, scorning him as much as she scorned herself, for she had been all too willing to forget that probability when Leo had come too close.

He vented a harsh laugh and raked his fingers through his luxuriant black hair. Tousled, those thick, sleek strands demonstrated a strong tendency to curl. So like Jake's hair that, momentarily, she ached just looking at him.

'"A sleazy roll in the hay",' he repeated with a darkly reflective look. 'Yet it is so very appealing a prospect when I am with you... Furthermore, I have not been in another woman's bed!'

Angie folded her arms in a jerky movement, devastated by how very personal things were getting at such mind-blowing speed. Meaning to walk out of the room but some-how finding herself glued to the carpet, she said, 'I don't believe you.'

'Would that I had had either the desire or the common sense to fulfil your expectation!' Leo ground out with wrathful emphasis. 'But from the minute I laid eyes on you last night I wanted you again, and I haven't yet sunk so low that I would try to dull that desire in any other bed— most especially not with a woman who deserves only my respect!'

Angie unravelled and absorbed that speech. She saw that she had already been allotted the blame for the reawakening of that sexual hunger. The eternal Eve, tempting and lur-ing—but Leo was no innocent and trusting Adam likely to be drawn blindly to destruction! And she could've done without the silent confirmation that she was not worthy of the same respect as the unknown woman he had spent so many hours with, in bed or otherwise. 'I hate you, Leo.'

'No, you don't. A little hatred would be a big help to us both right now,' Leo breathed with savage candour as he strode restively away from her, chiselled classic profile hard as iron. 'I didn't seek this attraction, but it is still there between us...'

'Is that your excuse for coming on to me like a bull in a china shop?' Angie whispered unsteadily.

Leo wheeled round, outraged black eyes glittering over her in a stormy arc. He hissed something in Greek.

Unimpressed, Angie gave him a look blistering with all the hatred he had so recently denied she could be feeling, but inside she still felt about an inch tall and sick to the stomach with humiliation. 'Because you thought I'd be easy; you thought all you had to do was take one look and stretch out a hand and say, "Let's go to bed," and I would naturally fall over myself to please. After all, you are *so* rich and *so* good-looking and *so* tremendous in bed that some lesser being like me who does other people's washing and cleaning wouldn't require any more taxing or charming approach from you!'

A blaze of dark colour fired over Leo's bold cheekbones. He spread both hands wide in front of him in a violent movement that sought to silence her. 'You are making me furious…and I can barely believe that you should dare to insult me like this!'

'That stupid teenager who thought she was calling all the shots got rings run round her two and a half years ago— and that is the lesson I learned best, Leo,' Angie informed him bitterly. 'I was nothing to you; I was just a body you used—'

He strode forward and settled two powerful hands on her slim shoulders. He was so enraged that she let out a startled yelp of fear, and his hands flew off her again as he gritted a sharp expletive and drew back from her. 'You twist the past so much, I don't recognise it on your lips…and don't you *dare* jump like that as if I'm about to hit you!' he roared down at her in angry reproach.

'Is it my fault you don't like the plain speaking you're so good at yourself?' Angie swiftly recovered the ground she had lost with that craven cry of fright.

'I know what is wrong with you now. You can't handle the fact that I should admit that I didn't want this attraction to be reborn,' Leo sliced back at her crushingly.

'From where I'm standing there *is* no attraction!'

'No?' Leo gave her a very dangerous look, redolent of a male well aware of his own powers of seduction.

'Just you stay away from me, Leo.'

'Is not the proof of the pudding in the eating?' Leo enquired thickly.

'You're furious with me right now,' Angie reminded him, because he appeared to be in need of that reminder.

'No man could stay angry with a woman who looks like you…'

'The king of the cliché too.'

Leo snaked out a long arm and closed it round her waist so fast that he gave a great shout of laughter when he saw her disconcerted face. 'Come to Brussels with me in the morning. Give me something to look forward to in the evenings—and I will look after you in every way you can think of…and in many that you probably can't,' he promised in a savouring tone of such intense desire that she shivered violently, exhaustion suddenly engulfing her as she struggled to react to his lightning-fast and disorientating change of mood.

'Dream on,' Angie advised raggedly, but even her weary pulses leapt as she met those brilliant dark eyes.

'Why fight me? Why pretend?' Leo demanded in equally sudden exasperation as he freed her again to stare down at her in brooding challenge. 'I am not suggesting a couple of stolen nights on the tiles… Stay with me until this burns out for both of us!'

And Angie recalled that day in the meadow by the lake when Leo had become bored with her girlish brand of teasing flirtation and had impatiently dragged her down into a passion which had far exceeded her naive expectations, swiftly, surely and ruthlessly overstepping the boundaries she had foolishly believed she could retain. When Leo wanted something, he wanted it yesterday. And, just below that sophisticated and cool cosmopolitan surface, Leo was as shockingly domineering and unashamedly primal in his appetites as a sixteenth-century pirate marauding the seven seas.

'No—and I won't say thank you for asking,' Angie muttered, but she was striving not to reel visibly from a proposition which had shaken her to her very depths.

'*Theos*, Angie,' Leo breathed grimly, his eloquent mouth curling. 'What more could you expect me to offer you now?'

Angie's paralysis gave and a sharp laugh empty of humour was dragged from her. She loathed Leo so much in that moment, she frankly marvelled that she did not succumb to physically attacking him. Neanderthal hypocrite, with his double standards, and proud of it! He thought she was a tart and a thief, didn't even trust her near his big fancy desk, so he wouldn't treat her as he might have treated any other woman.

'If I'd been interested, which I'm *not*,' she stressed with cloaked and embittered eyes, 'you might have just begun the way guys usually begin—you might just have asked me for a date—'

'A *date*?' Leo ejaculated with savage incredulity.

'Who knows? If you'd given me roses and poured enough champagne down my throat, and chatted me up with all that hypocrisy you consider beneath your exalted status, you might even have got lucky,' Angie framed with a suffocating, choking sense of injustice and wounded pride. 'As it is you just burnt out at supersonic speed, Leo. Congratulations!'

And with that last word Angie walked out of the library before the angry, scorching tears stinging her eyes overcame her in front of him.

Leo had certainly told her what he wanted from her—just sex, and the opportunity to rid himself of a lust for her body that was no more welcome to him now than it had been in the past. Gosh, that weekend must have been something special in his memory too! She had had nobody to compare him to then and nobody even now, and suddenly that reality infuriated her. All these wretched, mixed-up emotions tumbling around inside her, the terrible pain lurking ready to pounce at the very heart of that turmoil. Leo…Leo…Leo. Yet she knew she wanted him every bit as much as she hated him for not offering her more—so where did that leave her?

A determined hand shook her awake. Like a zombie, Angie fought to focus on the dark and forceful male features swimming above hers. 'Go away,' she groaned, closing her heavy eyes again.

The warm duvet was rolled back and Leo scooped her up into his arms before she could even register what was happening to her.

'What the heck are you doing?' she squawked.

'Bringing you down for breakfast.'

'Is there no food in the house?'

After a pause, the broad, muscular chest against which Leo had her firmly cradled rumbled with appreciative amusement. 'Funny…'

'What time is it?'

'Six—'

'Six?' Angie yelped as he carried her down the stairs with complete cool. 'That means I've only been in bed for a couple of hours!'

'I'm leaving for the airport at seven.'

'Go ahead; just put me back in bed before you go…and for heaven's sake put me down before you drop me!'

Leo lowered her down to the cold, tiled floor of the hall with a controlled strength that was deeply impressive, and finger-combed her tumbled hair back from her sleep-flushed face with an easy familiarity that shocked her back out of being impressed. But then plunging her into shock, she conceded dazedly, was what Leo had always excelled at.

Only during that stolen weekend had she learnt that Leo was a male of volatile temperament and intense passion. That cool, controlled front he wore to the world had been no more indicative of his true character than a one dimensional image. And that revelation, that shocking but joyous discovery of a fire that burned even hotter than her own, had sent Angie flying from the height of what had probably been infatuation down into the infinitely more dangerous and vulnerable depths of deep and very real love. From that point on, loving Leo had been a one-way ticket ever downward to hell, she acknowledged painfully.

'Why are you doing this to me?' she whispered tightly.

'I wanted to speak to you before I left.'

'Speak...'

In answer, Leo threw wide the dining-room door. 'We'll breakfast first.'

'I don't eat before I wash.'

'Unwashed, you look tousled and pink and sexy... I love it.'

Unnerved by that blatant admission and the scorchingly sensual smile that went with it, Angie raced back upstairs again and slammed the door on his laughter. Leo was advancing on her like an invading army on all fronts. Strange, wasn't it? When she had chased him up hill and down dale he had been most frustratingly elusive. But when she now attempted to do the sensible thing and run the other way Leo went into hot pursuit mode. But then no doubt it was Leo's natural drive to be the hunter rather than the quarry...and it certainly hadn't taken him long to turn the tables on her that weekend.

It took Angie precisely five minutes to wash her face and brush her teeth and dive into jeans and a sweatshirt. Jake was still soundly asleep. She stalked into the dining room and took a seat opposite Leo. As Epifania poured coffee into fine porcelain cups, Leo lounged back indolently in his carved dining chair, a vision of continental elegance in an exquisitely tailored navy suit and burgundy silk tie. He had all the dark and brooding magnificence of a Renaissance prince. Her pulse fluttered at the base of her throat like a trapped butterfly.

Awesomely aware of his level scrutiny, Angie refused the housekeeper's offer of a cooked breakfast and helped herself with a not quite steady hand to toast. The silence lingered until the door closed.

'I want your promise that you'll still be here when I return,' Leo said quietly then.

'To serve myself up on a platter to Wallace like the Christmas turkey? You have just got to be joking!'

Leo surveyed her steadily, and somehow that dark, piercing gaze made her squirm. 'He's a very old man who grew up in a radically different world and, whether or not you like to face it, you wronged him. You should have respect for his wish to meet his only great-grandchild. I confess that I myself was surprised that he should be prepared to express that wish.'

Angie was very tense. 'I'm sorry, but I'm not going.'

'I'm afraid I can't even offer Drew as bait,' Leo murmured with a curled lip.

Angie gave him an abstracted frown. 'Sorry?'

'My cousin won't be featuring in the seasonal festivities. Shortly after your departure, Wallace and Drew had an almighty row about his debts and a bitter parting of the ways,' Leo revealed wryly. 'Since then, Drew has been living in New York.'

Angie nodded, not really that surprised by the news. Drew Neville had lost his parents when he was ten, and Wallace had raised him to adulthood, fondly fulfilling his grandson's every desire, only to become outraged by the end result of that indulgence. He had expected Drew to take over the management of the estate, but Drew had demonstrated the strongest possible aversion to working for a living.

Indeed, battles over his extravagance and his laziness had been frequent and explosive. In Angie's time, however, Drew had still been coasting along fairly happily on an extremely generous allowance and the comfortable conviction that, as he had had the good fortune to be born in the direct male line, and not to a mere, insignificant daughter like Leo, he would one day inherit the Court and all it contained.

'No comment?'

Her brow furrowing, Angie met intent dark eyes and finally registered *why* Leo was treating her to that frowning scrutiny. Naturally, he had been expecting rather more of a reaction to his announcement that the supposed father of her child now lived way across the Atlantic!

Angie lowered her head and stared into her coffee cup. She could've kicked herself for not working out sooner that Drew *had* to be estranged from his family. How else could the belief that he was her son's father ever have arisen? After all, had Drew been on the spot to defend himself, he would soon have scotched any belief that there was the remotest chance that he could have had anything to do with Angie's pregnancy! And, all of a sudden, Angie felt quite weak with relief that Drew was thousands of miles away and out of touch. Had it been otherwise, she would not have been able to conserve her pride and save face by taking advantage of Leo's staunch conviction that Jake was his cousin's child.

'Frankly, after all this time, I couldn't care less where Drew lives. And certainly his absence, or indeed even his presence,' Angie went on daringly, 'wouldn't make the slightest difference to my determination not to go back to Deveraux Court.'

'But nonetheless you will go,' Leo told her very quietly.

There was something about that tone which sent a little ripple of apprehension down Angie's already taut spinal cord but irritably denying the impression, she forced a mocking smile. 'How? Are you planning to tie me up and stuff me in the boot of your car?'

Leo released his breath in an almost languorous sigh, spiky black lashes low on hooded dark eyes. 'Don't make me use pressure on you, Angie. I'm not in the habit of taking a sledgehammer to a nut but, if you push me, I'll shatter you into so many pieces you will find it a great challenge to put yourself together again.'

The blood slowly drained from Angie's shattered face. That silken, soft tone of threat had been infinitely more effective than an angry shout would have been. And the chilling scrutiny which went with it churned up her stomach. 'You can't intimidate me.'

'I believe I just did…and it shouldn't have been necessary,' Leo drawled. 'You *owe* Wallace at least one visit.'

'And where does that fit in with the pass you made at me last night?' Angie prompted in helpless confusion.

'It doesn't. You and I are one thing, and my grandfather and I another,' Leo informed her very drily. 'And at his age I think he's got to come first, don't you?'

CHAPTER FOUR

THE morning Leo was due back, Epifania bustled round the town house humming under her breath, so Angie sat in the beautifully landscaped back garden, glumly watching Jake gather gravel off the paths into tiny piles and transfer each stone individually into a bucket with the happy concentration of a little boy knowing he was getting thoroughly dirty.

She curled her chilled hands up inside her sleeves. Her one presentable outfit—a loose dark blue cotton jacket and matching short skirt—was more summer-weight than winter-weight. Her head was sore and her throat raw with the onset of a cold and, even in the sunlight and the shelter of the walls, she was freezing. And all she had to look forward to was a return to Deveraux Court, she reflected with an appalled shiver.

Wallace would get to meet his great-grandchild simply because she had less than five pounds to her name and was too much of a coward to face up to Leo's nebulous threat of retribution. Although really there hadn't been anything *remotely* nebulous about that threat, she reminded herself grimly. She had labelled herself a thief and she was aware that she could still be prosecuted. Naturally Leo would crack that whip of reality over her head. He hadn't had to spell out his meaning any more clearly.

And she had duly cringed and shuddered, not so much from the intimidation itself but from a stupid sense of savage shock and pain that Leo could turn those hard, dark, ice-cold eyes on her as he had and frighten the living daylights out of her without remorse.

He had phoned twice over the past few days. Angie had refused to speak to him. Epifania had been aghast at such

61

a rude response. Leo was her idol, and idols deserved ful-
some worship and appreciation. The housekeeper had been
very chatty until she'd finally appreciated that Angie didn't
want to hear generously offered little titbits about Leo from
the age of nought to thirty.

In fact the less Angie heard about Leo's wonderfully
idyllic childhood, genius-level brilliance and meteoric rise
to success and power in contrast to the deep and abiding
tragedies of his private life—death of his mother, his father,
his wife, his child—well, the safer she would be. Don't
feed an obsession, starve it to death, Angie had urged herself staunchly. She had stopped loving him years ago. Yet
somehow Leo *still* had the power to reach down inside her
and hurt her so deeply that he terrified her.

Leo paused to watch her where she perched on the ornate
bench, her mane of hair blowing back from her perfect
profile, slim shoulders taut, long, shapely legs crossed. His
strong, dark face instantly lightened and relaxed. Jake saw
him first, surging upright and hurtling across the gravel to
throw himself at Leo's knees. 'Waff man!' he cried excit-
edly.

It was hard to say which of them was most taken aback
by that unexpected welcome. Angie froze, but Leo froze
even more, his big, powerful body rigid. She saw into him
then. A male who genuinely loved children but who didn't
want anything to do with *her* child. Mean, nasty, she
thought painfully, and then Leo suddenly bent down to lift
Jake up and Jake, unable to distinguish strained pretence
from sincerity, flung his little arms round Leo and hugged
him tight.

'Put him down...' Just as suddenly, Angie could not bear
the knowledge and weight of her own pretence. Seeing father and son so close, and yet so far from each other in
their mutual ignorance of their true relationship, pierced her
like a guilty knife. Mean and nasty, she repeated afresh to
herself. Well, the lie that had made Jake's conception pos-

sible had been pretty mean and nasty too, she conceded heavily.

'Every time I look at him I think of you with Drew,' Leo admitted grimly as he settled the restive toddler in his arms gently back down onto solid earth. 'But that's not your son's fault, is it? And I hope I am man enough to recognise my own failings.'

'That old dog-in-the-manger feeling?' Angie questioned tartly, but a tiny betraying catch in her voice interfered with her delivery. 'I'm glad you recognise it as a failing...for you certainly didn't want me—'

'I didn't let you go to stand back and watch you make a bloody fool of yourself over my cousin!' Leo responded with biting censure.

'You didn't, *let me go*, Leo. You binned me like yesterday's newspaper.'

His even white teeth gritted. 'For a woman, you can be very blunt.'

'You taught me that.'

Drew again, Angie reflected bitterly. Leo was so certain that his cousin was Jake's father. He hadn't the slightest doubt—and suddenly she marvelled at that *absolute* certainty of his. Mightn't the average male have at least wondered whether there was a small possibility that her child might be his? No form of contraception was foolproof.

She cleared her throat, no longer able to deny her own dangerous curiosity to know how and in what manner Leo had first learnt of her pregnancy. 'When did Wallace tell you that I was pregnant?' she asked stiffly.

A winged black brow lifted. 'He didn't tell me...at least, not until I opened the subject with him.'

Angie frowned in confusion. 'Then *how*...?'

Leo dealt her an almost pitying look. 'It was Drew who couldn't wait to tell me. In fact, he boasted about his virility—'

'Drew *b-boasted*…?' Angie heard herself stammering in stunned disbelief.

Leo absorbed the beetroot-red flush of chagrin washing over her face but misunderstood its source. 'Presumably he felt it was safe to own up. By then you had been gone several weeks…and I believe he gave you the money for an abortion. No doubt he believed that that would be the end of the episode.'

Angie was very still, and then her tremulous mouth compressed rock-hard and she dropped her head. She marvelled that she didn't explode with sheer outrage, for no longer did she need to wonder at Leo's unquestioning acceptance that Jake was another man's child. His cousin's confession, his cousin's crude, cruel *lies*, evidently couched in the most offensive male terms, had ensured Leo's conviction. For if Drew had accepted responsibility and even pretended that he had offered her the money for a termination as a send-off, what normal, rational male would then doubt the paternity of the unborn child involved?

'If it's any consolation, I hit him,' Leo informed her lazily.

'You hit him…?' Angie framed weakly, still numb with fury at the betrayal of someone she had considered a friend, and unable at that moment to even begin to understand why Drew should have done such a crazy thing. She snatched in a deep, shuddering breath. 'If he's still alive, you didn't hit him hard enough!'

The silence thundered and then Leo flung back his arrogant dark head and laughed with earthy appreciation.

Startled by that disorientating response, Angie glanced up. She saw Leo as she had so often seen him that long-ago weekend—shorn of all cool reserve and distance, and utterly irresistible. The breathtakingly charismatic smile slashing his hard, dark features stopped her heart dead in its tracks. Her breathing quickening, Angie simply stared, helpless as a bird caught in the hunter's net.

Then Leo glanced down at his watch, faint impatience drawing his black brows together as he registered the time. 'We'll leave for the Court as soon as you're ready.'

Dragged back down to reality and ashamed of every leaping sense that sought to betray her, Angie stood up. 'I'll never forgive you for forcing me to go back there.'

'Occasionally one has to be cruel to be kind,' Leo said drily. 'If you had been foolish enough to do a disappearing act while I was away, I might not have been able to find you again.'

Angie wasn't listening; she was already picturing the horrors of humiliation awaiting her. Return of the prodigal, but not to a feast of celebration. Wallace would meet his great-grandson, even if the paternity of that great grandson was not quite what he apparently imagined it to be. And her father was either in for a heck of a nasty shock or presently praying nightly that his scarlet woman of a daughter would not dare to show her face again and embarrass him. Jake's illegitimacy would be as big a badge of public shame in Samuel Brown's eyes as it would be in his elderly employer's.

However, her exposure as the household thief would've been an even greater sin to a man whose unswerving devotion to the Neville family, their every minute interest and their ancestral home was so extreme, he would probably have handed his daughter over to the police personally had he found her with that miniature portrait in her possession.

'Angie…?'

Angie swallowed hard on the thickness in her throat. 'I think you owe me one favour, Leo. I want you to promise me that as soon as this wretched visit is over you'll fix me up with a job somewhere.'

'You won't need a job. Your future is already assured. Either I will keep you or Wallace will keep you.'

'Nobody needs to keep me, Leo.'

'My offer is open any time you want to take it up.'

She spun away, jumpy as a cat on hot bricks. 'You're astonishingly persistent.'

Leo laced long, lean fingers into several strands of her pale hair and tugged her head gently back to him. Raw desire blazed in his bold dark eyes. 'Hungry...very, very hungry,' he corrected her without shame.

That close to him, Angie trembled, her nostrils flaring on the clean, warm male scent, so distinctively his and as addictive as a drug to her. That same hunger thundered through every fibre of her being without conscience. She could no more have denied his power over her than she could have denied her need to breathe, but when her awareness shrank to the lustrous brilliance of those spectacular eyes she knew that her own physical weakness would tear her apart at the seams if she wasn't careful.

Leo looked nothing short of spectacular in a superb double-breasted navy pinstripe suit which outlined every honed angle of his magnificent physique. Just four and a half days he had been away, but it had felt like a lifetime to Angie. The urge to accept that wretched phone just to hear that deep, dark, rich drawl had tormented her, *shamed* her. Her nails carved sharp crescents into her moist palms as she balled her hands into defensive fists because she wanted so badly to touch him.

Leo inclined his dark head, lean fingers rising to tilt her chin so that he could look at her. 'You look so bloody haunted and miserable...anybody would think I have insulted you!' he condemned with suppressed savagery. 'I am expressing a need openly, honestly, but I won't promise you anything I won't deliver, and at the end of it I will leave you and your son secure. You want the roses and the champagne, I'll give them to you—but all I want from you is *you*.'

Angie twisted her pounding head away. 'Back off, Leo.'

'I don't know how... I have hardly slept since I left

London... I was *angry* with you! We could have been together in Brussels—'

'Yes... A few days is about the limit of your attention
span as I recall—'

With a stifled expletive, Leo gathered her into his arms
and brought his mouth down on hers, all explosive fire and
frustration. Her head spun and her lower limbs shook, and
the heat of her own treacherous craving stormed through
her chilled flesh, leaving her weak and pliable and yet oh,
so hot, oh, so sensitive that her skin felt as if it was burning
up. Moaning deep in her throat beneath the erotically in-
vasive thrust of his tongue, she clung to him with the same
desperation with which she might have clung to the edge
of a cliff.

And then a little hand tugged at her nylon-covered thigh,
demanding attention, and Jake said insistently, 'Mummy?'
and the effect was as good as a bucket of icy water thrown
over her racing pulses and madly accelerated heartbeat.

In one charged motion, Leo released her and stepped
back, a dull flush across his high cheekbones. Jake gazed
up at his mother in frank curiosity, and then he gazed up
at the tall, dark Greek towering over him. Angie gave her
son a shaky smile and, satisfied, he finally toddled off again
back to his bucket and his gravel.

'I forgot that we were not alone,' Leo murmured in a
distant tone, and his accent was very thick.

'Please don't touch me like that again.' Angie didn't
even trust herself enough to look at him, not when her body
still screamed and pulsed with guilty, wicked, unsated excitement. 'I want you to stay away from me.'

'Impossible. I'm driven by a very powerful need to possess you again.'

'But I won't be possessed ever again by you!' Angie
blazed up at him with explosive abruptness.

'You can fight me...but can you keep on fighting yourself as well?' Leo enquired with lethal effect.

Paling in fear of the merciless insight behind that question, Angie spun away, snatched up her son—who vented a startled chorus of complaint—and stalked back into the house.

After washing Jake's hands and dusting him down, she closed her suitcase and hauled it off the bed. She searched her face in the mirror, dwelling accusingly on her swollen mouth and the vulnerable brightness in her eyes. You fall by the wayside again, you deserve everything you suffered before and *worse*, she warned her reflection. Yet in some secretive, shameful way the raw strength of Leo's desire excited her and encouraged her thoughts to fly off in dangerous directions. Was it possible that Leo might actually have regretted that rejection two and a half years ago? Six weeks after that weekend they had spent together, Leo had returned to the Court for a flying visit...

He had climbed out of his glossy limousine in the rear courtyard, watching her pick her way across the cobbles in spindly heels and a tiny satin slip dress. The hand she had been resting on Drew's arm to balance herself had then chosen to cling in a possessive display, and she had tossed her hair back and smiled brilliantly.

'Hi, Leo!' she had called, all brave and bright and unconcerned, walking past as if he were just anyone, instead of the man who had torn her heart in two and left her more dead than alive.

And when she had come home in the early hours of the following morning, still dying that murderously slow death of deprivation inside herself, the party-girl façade abandoned for lack of an audience, Leo had strolled out through the French windows in the south wing and blocked her path.

'You're messing up your life, Angie.'

He had sounded horribly like her father, and she had treated him to an appropriately bored smile of indifference. 'If I am, I'm having a lot of fun, Leo.'

'What an incredible thrill it must be to play nightly chauffeur to a drunk.'

'Drew's not a drunk...he just likes to have a good time, that's all,' she had protested, defending the young man she had come to rely on as her only real friend. 'He takes me to parties and clubs, and I'm meeting a lot of people. In fact I'm having the most wonderful time I've ever had in my life! So what's that to you? What do you want from me?'

Given that foolish invitation to be frank, Leo's dark eyes had glittered like black ice in the moonlight. 'Nothing. Absolutely and finally nothing,' he had drawled with brutal conviction. 'What could I possibly want that I haven't already had? Sorry, but I don't go for the new look, Angie. That is a very trashy dress.'

And she had stood there for a very long time after he had gone, mascara-smeared round eyes emptied of tears, lipstick smudged, provocative dress lurching off one bowed shoulder, brave and bright no longer, doused like an already spent and flickering candle flame by his contemptuous distaste. She had known then that she would not tell Leo she was carrying his baby. She had known then that no matter how scared she was, no matter how desperate, she would never again allow Leo the opportunity to look down at her as if she were something that had just crawled up out of the gutter at his feet.

'You'll get over him,' Drew had said bracingly on one of the rare occasions when he was sober enough to make rational conversation. 'You had a crush and he just broke out of months of enforced celibacy. Don't build it into something it wasn't. I did try to warn you, didn't I? Leo's been chased the length and the breadth of two countries since he was a teenager. He's had besotted secretaries spread themselves across his desk, pornographic invitations from complete strangers and gorgeous lookers risking life and limb to attract his attention everywhere he goes...

Angie, you're lovely, but, sadly, there's a whole host of even lovelier women out there. You never had a hope of holding Leo.'

Drew had been so honest with her then. He had just told it as it was. Fact of life. Like to like. Leo would inevitably love and marry another rich, spoilt woman who would spend half the day complaining about a broken nail, the suspicion of a draught or the damp English climate which made her hair flop. In short, Leo would wed another Petrina, a self-obsessed, whinging moan...

'Shall I take your case down now, Miss Brown?'

Angie whipped round, scarlet with discomfiture, as if that last thought might be written in block capitals across her face. Leo's chauffeur was hovering expectantly outside the bedroom door. As she nodded and turned away to lift her son, she thought about Drew again and finally conceded that she had been foolish to trust him as a friend and confidant.

Drew had grown up the apple of his grandfather's eye, only to then find himself subjected to constant unflattering comparisons with Leo. As a result, Drew had learned to loathe Leo. And Drew must have sensed Leo's vein of lingering sexual possessiveness where the butler's daughter was concerned. The younger man could only have claimed an intimate relationship with Angie out of some hateful male competitive need to get a rise out of his cousin.

But she was still appalled that Drew, whom she had trusted with the secret of her pregnancy, could have sunk so low the minute she was out of sight and hearing. As for him giving her money towards an abortion...complete rubbish! Angie had never at any stage considered that possibility because Jake's conception had not been an accident. She could not have lived with that truth and gone on to contemplate a termination.

And perhaps she shouldn't have been so shocked by Leo's revelations, she acknowledged ruefully. She should have remembered that although there had never been anything but platonic friendship between her and Drew, although she had never been less than honest about her feelings for Leo, Drew had still stormed off in a furious sulk when she'd made the mistake of telling him that she was carrying Leo's baby.

Leo frowned at Angie's appearance as she descended the stairs, Jake anchored on her hip. '*Cristos*…it's the middle of winter out there!' he exclaimed. 'You'll freeze in that outfit. I assumed that you were changing into something more appropriate.'

Angie reddened with considerable embarrassment. 'It's either this or my jeans, and I happen to think I look smarter dressed like this.'

'We'll stop and buy you a coat on the way,' Leo said drily, as if he were talking to a very small and silly child.

'No. We will not stop anywhere and buy me *anything*,' Angie stressed, bright blue eyes spitting angry, defiant pride. 'I hope I know enough to be very, very wary of Greeks bearing gifts!'

Stunned by that acid retaliation, Leo froze. His aggressive jawline squared, anger flaring in his gleaming dark eyes. 'You insult me—'

'Isn't it strange how sensitive you can be when you're so very *in*sensitive about my feelings?' Angie slotted in between furiously clenched teeth.

Nostrils flaring, all volatile Greek in that instant, Leo flung wide the front door. Untouched by the wariness most individuals employed around Leo when he was in the wrong mood, Angie stalked down the steps, head held high, and climbed into the limousine. There she settled Jake into the brand-new child's car seat anchored opposite. It had obviously been purchased purely for her son's use…

However, new clothes for herself were one thing, her child's comfort and safety quite another. As Leo folded himself in beside her like a prowling sabre-toothed tiger, Angie said precisely nothing about the car seat. Indeed she turned her head rigidly away from him and stared blindly into space.

Angie woke up groggily, her cheek pillowed on a hard male thigh, her fingers loosely resting on another. Registering that she was virtually in Leo's lap, and that the warm, heavy weight round her shoulders was his arm, she turned scarlet, and in her haste to detach herself from him she very nearly catapulted herself onto the floor of the limousine.

Steadying herself perilously on the very edge of the seat, she pushed her tumbled hair back off her brow and thrust herself back into her former position in the opposite corner to do up the belt which Leo must have undone. Jake was asleep, baby-sized, breathy little snores emerging from him.

'He was marvellous company until about twenty minutes ago,' Leo remarked, grimly amused dark eyes absorbing her tousled discomfiture. 'You wouldn't believe how many cows, sheep and horses there are to exclaim over in the space of a hundred and fifty miles—'

'For heaven's sake, what time is it?' Angie looked at her watch in horror, registering that she had been asleep for almost two hours. It was late afternoon. Electric tension filled her as she appreciated that they would very shortly be reaching their destination.

'We saw a train too; that was a major highlight of our journey,' Leo continued silkily. 'But the memory I will cherish most was Jake's request for an urgent pit stop at the precise moment we *passed* the motorway services. The next fifteen miles went by in a blur of edge-of-the-seat excitement—'

'You had to take him to the toilet...why on earth didn't you wake me up?' Angie gasped in stricken embarrassment.

'You were dead to the world, and I was feeling generous.'

The back of Angie's nose tickled unbearably and she started sneezing. She fumbled for a tissue even though she knew she didn't have one. A pristine folded linen handkerchief was tossed on her lap.

'Thanks,' she mumbled round the fifth sneeze, and then she held her breath, hoping that it worked for sneezes the way it worked for hiccups. It didn't. Choking and spluttering, she began coughing instead. 'S-sorry...I seem to have caught a cold.'

'You can go straight to bed as soon as we arrive.'

'Do you think I could stay there until the New Year?' Angie asked facetiously because her heart was sinking like a stone with every mile that brought them closer to Deveraux Court.

'Take me with you and you'll be lucky to see daylight before the spring.'

Angie swallowed the next cough and shot him a startled glance.

Leo gazed back at her, his sensual mouth curving into a sudden slashing smile of vibrant amusement. Her drowsy eyes widened and, powerless to drag her attention from him again, she stared. Whoosh... That smile, full of such utterly mesmeric charm, dug talons into her heart. She had seen so much of that smile that long ago weekend...

It isn't just sex on his side, she had told herself then, buoyant with relief and optimism. He likes me, he understands my jokes, he looks so happy just to be with me. Angie stiffened at the recollection, the dreamy look in her eyes hardening into bitter self-reproach. She had really *believed* that Leo was feeling the same intense emotional sense of recognition that she was feeling. In between frantic bouts of sex, of course, she affixed painfully. She whipped her head round so abruptly to look out of the window that she hurt her neck.

And as she recognised the road her heart started beating suffocatingly fast behind her ribcage. Minutes later, the

limousine drove beneath the turreted gates of Deveraux
Court and up the thickly wooded, winding drive. Angie sat
forward, taut as a piece of elastic drawn too tight and ready
to break, imagery as sharp as needles stabbing at her and
tearing at the breath in her throat.

'Relax, Angie,' Leo advised lazily. 'You're coming
home.'

Home? Yes; painful and ironic as it was to remember,
she had once loved this place more than any other on earth.
She watched the vista of the parkland opening up, the rolling acres of the estate adorned by mature and stately trees,
beautiful even without the softening veil of spring leaves.
Then the drive rounded the last bend and the house itself
unfolded, an architectural triumph of elaborate but wonderfully time-mellowed Elizabethan brick.

The limo crunched across the gravel frontage and rolled
to a halt. Angie only had eyes now for the imposing front
door.

Sleepily stretching, Jake woke up and crowed in delight
as Leo unclasped the belt on the car seat and lifted him
into his arms.

Angie didn't even notice. For once she was blind and
deaf to her child as she slid out of the car and began walking slowly towards the door. She saw her father waiting, a
slight, dapper man in his early sixties, clad in an old-
fashioned dark suit. He looked so stiff, so unyielding, she
thought in sudden familiar pain, as if someone had sown
in a poker where his backbone should have been.

'Dad...?' she began unevenly.

'Good afternoon, madam...sir,' Samuel Brown murmured without any expression at all and the slight bow of
the head that he always practised around those people he
saw as his social superiors. 'I hope you had a good journey
down from town. A pleasant, fresh afternoon, isn't it?'

Angie was frozen to the spot. At that greeting, even Leo
stilled for a split second. Then he freed a hand from the

child clinging to his shoulder and rested it against Angie's tense back. 'Brown—?'

'Mr Neville is awaiting your arrival, sir,' her father continued with wooden precision. 'Do you wish me to show your guests upstairs first?'

'When the time comes, I shall conduct my guests upstairs, Brown,' Leo drawled with ice-cold clarity, long, lean fingers eloquent of his incredulity flexing against Angie's quivering spine. 'We will see my grandfather immediately but there is no need for you to announce us.'

'As you wish, sir,' the butler said punctiliously, and then he turned away to allow them through the door.

CHAPTER FIVE

As SAMUEL BROWN trod, rigid-backed, back across the echoing Great Hall and vanished beyond the green baize door below the magnificent Jacobean staircase, Angie gazed after her father, utterly savaged by his behaviour.

Leo lowered Jake to the floor. 'Wallace will be in the drawing room.'

'Don't you dare try to pretend that what just happened *didn't* happen!' Tears of distress lashed Angie's eyes. 'Did either you or Wallace even consider how my father might react to this situation?'

'I feel desperately sorry for a man who feels he has to go to such ridiculous lengths to demonstrate his disapproval,' Leo drawled with sardonic bite. 'But that little scene was pure, outrageous farce!'

'Dad doesn't think I belong here in this part of the house... In fact he obviously doesn't want me anywhere under this roof, and whose fault is that?'

'Drew's,' Leo slotted in grimly. 'And to a very large extent your own. Your relationship with your father was strained even before you left.'

'It's always been strained,' Angie muttered with driven honesty. 'Just you try inheriting a father who is a total stranger at the age of thirteen and see how you get on!'

'Brown will come round...he has no other choice,' Leo asserted with chilling conviction, his strong jawline hardening.

'Don't you dare say anything to him...don't you dare humiliate him like that!' Angie warned him fiercely, her anxiety on her parent's behalf palpable. 'I don't care if he treats me like the invisible woman; I can live with that. But don't you *dare* interfere, Leo. He has a private life and a family, and neither are any of your business!'

In fascination, Leo scanned her passionately defensive face. '*Theos*…you are deeply attached to your father.'

Having wearied of yanking at Leo's trouser leg for attention, the forgotten toddler hovering at their feet threw his little arms extravagantly wide and howled mournfully, 'Cuddle, Leo!'

Dredged from her self-preoccupation, Angie stared down at her child with a dropped jaw.

'Want cuddle,' Jake said less stridently, sidling up against Leo's knees and looking up at him pleadingly. 'Want carried.'

Angie tugged her son towards her, but he resisted every step of the way. 'Want Leo,' he told her stubbornly, stunning his mother with that bluntly stated preference.

'He's just not used to men,' she said in a rush. 'George Dickson was barely home long enough to notice his own kids, never mind one extra. I'm sorry.'

'Why should you apologise? Jake and I got to know each other while you were asleep.'

'I just didn't want him bothering you,' Angie muttered half under her breath.

'I like children…and I'm not proud of my initial response to your son. Do try not to keep on ramming it down my throat,' Leo urged with immense irritation.

But all over again Angie was seeing her son throw his arms wide in emphasis, spreading his little hands demonstratively in a direct and strikingly apt imitation of Leo's expressive body language. The sight had sent Angie's nervous tension rocketing sky-high. Guilt and a powerful current of dismay had seized her. Wallace Neville was a very shrewd old man. Suppose he saw that resemblance and exposed the charade she had allowed to continue? But wasn't it even more probable that he might simply take one astonished look at Jake's dark colouring and angrily proclaim his disbelief that his blond, blue-eyed grandson could possibly have fathered a child who looked so little like him?

Leo thrust open the door of the drawing room. Taut with apprehension, Angie preceded him, clutching her son's hand. Leo's grandfather stood in front of the fire, one frail hand braced on a walking stick, but his upright carriage, the proud set of his white head and the eagle-eyed sharpness of his gaze defied his eighty-odd years.

Angie hovered. Leo prodded her forward and closed the door. As Wallace Neville studied the little boy dragging his hand free of his mother's to run across to the huge wolfhound rising drowsily from the hearth, the most electrifying silence held. Then, as Angie began to move forward in dismay at Jake's headlong charge at the animal the old man raised an abrupt hand to stay her.

'Boris loves children, and the boy is fearless. You should be proud of him.'

As the wolfhound dropped obligingly back down on the rug so that it could rub its great head against Jake's chest, Angie stilled. 'I am,' she said rather defensively.

Wallace surveyed child and dog for several tense moments, and then he murmured with apparent satisfaction, 'He's a fetching little fellow with a strong look of the family about him. What do you think, Leo?'

Angie gulped and stopped breathing.

'He's an attractive child,' Leo conceded without voicing an opinion.

'I know a Neville nose when I see one,' his grandfather asserted as he pulled the bell rope by the massive fireplace. 'Precious little escapes these eyes of mine.'

Angie stiffened. But Wallace Neville turned back to her with a bland smile. 'You've done well to raise him this long alone, Angie. It couldn't have been easy.'

Angie swallowed uneasily, wondering if it was madness to imagine that that smile had a curious shark-like quality when she was being greeted with infinitely greater courtesy than she had ever expected to receive. 'It wasn't.'

'Well, that's over with now. Your life is about to change,' Wallace informed her.

'I'm not sure I want my—'

'I'm really looking forward to having a young child in the house over Christmas,' Wallace continued heartily as if he hadn't heard her. 'The festive season just isn't the same once the family all grow up.'

Angie was briefly sidetracked by that unexpected burst of sentiment. Christmas at Deveraux Court...how drab the season had seemed spent anywhere else, she conceded ruefully. Mistletoe and holly strung up round the Great Hall, the giant tree felled on the estate itself, the party for the staff...

'You'll wish to freshen up before dinner,' Wallace told her, springing her back out of her memories and making her tense up again. 'I hope you'll be very comfortable here, Angie. You ought to be...we've brought in a nanny to help out.'

'A nanny?' Angie exclaimed incredulously.

'Harriet Davis used to work for one of our neighbours and comes with excellent references.' Wallace nodded approvingly to himself. 'She's fairly panting with eagerness to get her hands on this little chap.'

As Angie parted her lips to voice her objections to such an arrangement being made without recourse to her, the door opened and the rotund and decidedly determined-looking shape of Nanny Davis swam into view. She gave Angie a wide, excited smile, but her attention swung almost immediately to the child kneeling beside the wolfhound.

'Oh, what a little pet,' she carolled with warm appreciation. 'What a portrait that would make, sir!'

'Nanny's going to keep an eye on us both while Jake and I become acquainted,' Wallace announced, exercising the same prerogative as royalty in concluding the interview the instant it had served his purpose.

Leo curved a lean hand round Angie's elbow and pressed her out of the room. 'Jake won't come to any harm,' he said as he absorbed her angry disconcertion. 'And you can't be tied night and day to a toddler's demands while you're here. I'll show you to your room.'

'Now that you have divested me of my child...mission accomplished, is that it?' Angie accused as she followed him up the stairs.

'If my mission had been accomplished...' Leo paused on the minstrel's gallery to wait for her, densely lashed dark eyes scanning her beautiful face and flaring to hot gold. '...I wouldn't still be seething with lust.'

Angie's heartbeat hit the Richter scale as her eyes clashed with that smouldering, explicit look. A frisson of treacherous heat slivered through her tensing limbs, and she trembled. 'Leo—'

'On the other hand, satisfaction didn't lead to satiation the last time,' Leo conceded in a throaty purr of intimate recollection. 'I couldn't get enough of you. And you couldn't get enough of me. No man could possibly forget a reception like that.'

Angie went scarlet with shame at the reminder, but her breasts still stirred and swelled inside her cotton bra, her nipples peaking into taut, achingly sensitive buds.

'And if I want to experience that all over again who could blame me?' Leo murmured softly. 'You would be a liar if you pretended to be any less eager. And why *should* you lie? There's no disgrace in acknowledging sexual hunger...or in satisfying it.'

Angie snatched in a tremulous breath and looked away, a hot pink flush delineating her cheekbones. Leo made it sound so easy, so simple. Sex as a mere bodily appetite, a hunger to assuage. He foresaw no complications. But then why should he? The very ease with which she had once surrendered her body had strongly influenced Leo's opinion of her. But Leo was a dangerously unpredictable mix of two very different cultures. He could sound so liberal, but he was fundamentally Greek and he hadn't loved or married a woman with permissive values. Drew had been very snide about the lack of intimacy between Leo and Petrina before their wedding...

'It tells you so much about the *real* Leo,' Drew had sneered. 'He's no more British in his attitudes than an alien! He had a load of hot affairs, but when it came to settling down he went back home and chose a prissy little Greek girl with a padlock on her virtue!'

The recollection made Angie flush uncomfortably. Belatedly registering that she had been dawdling and that Leo was subjecting her to a questioning appraisal while he waited for her to catch up, she parted her lips and asked jerkily, 'Where am I sleeping...the attics?'

In answer, Leo strolled forward and cast the door wide on the magnificent Chinese bedroom suite. Drawing level with him, Angie stilled on the threshold, stealing a shocked and intimidated glance over the exquisite hand-blocked wallpaper and the delicate antique satinwood suite of furniture, which complemented the ornate four-poster bed with its superbly embroidered drapes and gilded and domed canopy lined with pleated scarlet silk. Then, straightening her back, she stepped over the invisible line of unease which had briefly gripped her.

'Go to bed for a while before dinner,' Leo urged almost gently.

The instant she was alone, Angie inched forward almost guiltily onto the rich expanse of the oriental rug. Through the connecting door lay a grand Edwardian bathroom and dressing room. This was the south wing, which housed the principal guest rooms. Built in the late eighteenth century, a tribute to classical elegance, the south wing provided a radical contrast to the dark, oak-panelled rooms of the original Tudor house.

Her father and stepmother lived in the basement of the north wing, which was only about a hundred and fifty years old, but ironically that final Victorian addition to the Court had proved to be the least resistant to the cruel ravages of time...

'A dark, dank little hole of a place,' Angie's mother, Grace, had called it with a shudder of contemptuous distaste. 'I couldn't believe that your father expected me to live in a dump like that!'

The break between her parents had been bitter and final. Her mother had gone for a divorce and she had never looked back. A qualified caterer, she had started up her own restaurant and Angie had been attending an exclusive boarding-school by the age of seven. Only then had Grace told her daughter that the father she had never met was a butler, but that it had to be a big secret because her school-friends would laugh at her if they ever found out.

In short, Angie had been brought up to be ashamed of both her father and his means of making a living. But when Angie was thirteen her mother had died very suddenly of a heart attack and, simultaneously, Samuel Brown had become an unavoidable element of his teenage daughter's life.

The restaurant and the apartment above it had been mortgaged to the hilt. Grace had lived well and died at forty-two, and she hadn't prepared for that possibility. Angie had had to leave her expensive fee-paying school. In the space of one shattering month, she had been forced to relinquish everything familiar and secure, and she had moved to Devon to attend a local school and live at Deveraux Court.

Like a too brightly coloured and strident parrot, she had swooped into her father and stepmother's bland lives, her habits, her expectations, her very outlook and image of herself utterly foreign and threatening to theirs. Their damp little flat had appalled her and, like her mother before her, she had had little respect for her father's unswerving loyalty to an old man who paid him so little that even his best suit was patched.

The discovery that her father had recently remarried *had* initially been a shock, but timid, rather colourless little Emily had been no wicked stepmother. The middle-aged daughter of a retired estate worker, and as indoctrinated with the tradition of serving the Nevilles as her butler husband, Emily had seemed the perfect wife, tailor-made for a man of Samuel's old-fashioned ilk...

Chewing uncomfortably at her lower lip, Angie hunched her shoulders beneath her jacket, thinking uneasily about her stepmother, a woman she had never really got to know until it was too late. She stared out of the window towards the distant boundaries of the ancient woodland which she had once loved with a passion only equalled by the love she had learnt to feel for the house itself. The Court was like an ever expanding time capsule, crammed full of wonderful, personal reminders of all the people who had ever lived within its walls right down through the ages.

But about four years ago some of those wonderful and irreplaceable items had begun to go missing, Angie recalled painfully. First a small brass carriage clock and, shortly afterwards, a little silver manicure set, both taken from rarely used bedrooms. Then the thefts had entered a new phase, the articles clearly picked for their infinitely greater value. A Dresden shepherdess, a pair of exquisite matching salt-cellars, a Georgian tea caddy in the shape of a pear...

'It has to be someone with easy access to the house,' the police had told Wallace.

All the staff had been grilled repeatedly. Angie herself had been interviewed twice over. As her father had discovered and announced each fresh disappearance, the entire household had gone into uproar. Suspicion had divided everybody into uneasy camps. For weeks, Samuel Brown had prowled about at night, hoping to catch the culprit. He had responded to those thefts as if he had personally failed in his duty towards his employer. And nobody, not a single one of them, had once, to Angie's knowledge, even begun to suspect the person whom Angie had ultimately found in possession of that miniature...

Angie had been shattered, too, but desperately keen to mount a cover-up. She had rushed to replace the miniature before its absence could be noted. But Wallace had surprised her with the tiny portrait still clasped in her hand, and had naturally assumed that she'd been stealing it. Angie had appreciated too late the risk she had run.

Downstairs today, Wallace had betrayed not an ounce of recollection of that previous humiliating encounter. But Angie would never forget that instant of being caught, the old man's shock and outrage and the terror which had made her proclaim her pregnancy. She shook her head to clear it of the unpleasant memory, and focused then on the three figures walking slowly towards the stable block in the fading light. Wallace and her son, Nanny Davis bringing up the rear.

With a sigh, Angie sank down on the edge of the bed, feeling her own superfluity. But since she couldn't imagine Leo's grandfather dining in the messy presence of a toddler—and that same toddler would by that hour be ready only for bed, yet still in need of careful supervision in so large and unfamiliar a house—perhaps Leo had been right about her needing some help. More right certainly, it seemed, than he had been about Wallace requiring her to grovel...

Her head was heavy. Deciding that she might as well lie down for a while, Angie undressed down to her bra and pants. She studied the fire burning in the marble fireplace. Such luxury for the butler's daughter—but then she was really stealing a ride on her son's bandwagon, she reminded herself ruefully. After carefully rolling back the opulent bedspread, she slid between the crisp, laundered sheets.

Wallace had outlived his own children, become estranged from one grandson and endured the death of his first great-grandchild, Leo's baby daughter. Now he was prepared to welcome Jake into his home in spite of the manner of his birth. Why was it that she wasn't wholly convinced by Wallace's change of heart? Her son was the old man's flesh and blood, and the passage of time could work miracles...

Only not when it came to her response to Leo, Angie affixed in stark shame. No, nothing had changed there. Leo looked at her and she still burned. She pressed her hot face into the cool of the pillow, but it couldn't ease her growing apprehension. One moment of weakness and she would put both herself and her son in an intolerable—indeed, unthinkable—position.

A small sound woke Angie up, sending her eyes flying wide. A lamp by the bed had been lit, the curtains pulled. Leo was poised by the fire, a brooding frown on his strong, dark face. It was there, and then it was gone the instant he met her startled eyes, his vibrantly handsome features smoothing back into impassivity.

'What are you doing in here?' Angie whispered shakily.

'I came to see how you were and stayed to replenish the fire.'

'I'm feeling OK,' Angie lied tautly, having been brought up to believe that it was bad manners to admit to not feeling well in the company of others.

'You don't look it. I suggest you give dinner a miss and remain in bed.'

Abruptly, Angie sat up. 'Oh, that would make a great impression on your grandfather, wouldn't it? The guest who arrived and took straight to her bed like a dying swan!'

'Jake is a major hit. I don't think you need to worry about the impression you might be making.'

'I wasn't worrying.' Her voice was tart because she hated it when Leo saw her weaknesses and insecurities.

'You've been jumping at your own shadow ever since you arrived,' Leo traded, unimpressed. 'Peace and quiet might soothe your nerves—'

'I don't have nerves!'

'You have them all over every inch of that exquisitely responsive body, and in some of the most truly entrancing and unexpected places,' Leo countered with indolent cool, glittering dark eyes anchored without remorse to the colour rising in her cheeks as he strolled round to the side of the bed.

'Stay away from me!' Angie warned half an octave higher as she scrambled across the mattress in the other direction.

Leo stilled to look reflectively down at her. 'Is this another game, *pethi mou*?'

'I don't know what you're talking about.'

'All the virginal screeching and evasive manoeuvres.'

Angie's unsteady hands clenched hard. 'I just don't want to get involved with you again.'

Leo loosened his jacket and sank fluidly down onto the edge of the bed. 'Did I hurt you so much?' he enquired softly, casually, making it intimidatingly obvious that he was in complete control. 'You bit off rather more than you could chew with me, Angie. Isn't that the truth? Two and a half years ago you wanted to tease and play, and I yanked the rug from beneath your feet and took more than I believe you ever intended to give.'

'Shut up, Leo!' Angie flopped back down against the pillows, her eyes over-bright, her soft mouth tremulous with pain.

'I ask you now...what did you expect from a man who had buried both his wife and his child only months earlier and who was still haunted by his memories and his conscience?' Leo continued levelly. 'I wanted to be alone and you crowded me. You forced me to notice you and, in some ways, I hated you for that. But even then I couldn't deny that I wanted you too.'

'All I want now is for you to leave me alone!'

Leo ran a caressing forefinger down over the taut, slim fingers clutching the sheet, and she snatched her hand out of reach as if the warm touch of his skin had scorched her. 'You've learnt to be wary...you're scared this time—'

'I'm not scared!'

'No?' Leo gazed down at her steadily, and her world shrank to the drowning darkness of his spectacular eyes. 'Then why do you behave like a frightened child every time I come close?'

'That's rubbish...'

Leo laced long brown fingers slowly into a hank of pale blonde hair and, with his other hand, drew her inexorably up to him. Her heart was banging like clashing cymbals against her taut ribcage. She could hardly get breath into her lungs for she knew that if he touched her she was lost, and yet she could not summon up the strength to break away from him.

'You're all woman, Angie...you melt in my arms,' he breathed caressingly. 'That is how it should be...'

Alarm bells rang in Angie's head. 'Like heck it is...it's blasted dangerous!'

'Safe things can be very boring,' Leo told her thickly as he lowered his dark, arrogant head and pressed his mouth with raw, driving hunger to hers.

She fell into that kiss like a starving woman at a banquet. Anguished desire stormed through her, and suddenly her arms were opening and reaching up, finding his broad shoulders, rejoicing in the hard muscles and the heat she could feel through his jacket. Pulses racing, heartbeat thundering in her eardrums, her own need rose up inside her and overflowed with devastating effect.

Leo gave a growl of satisfaction and rolled over, hauling

the sheet out of his path to pull her fully into his arms, one powerful hand curving round a slender hip to press her into contact with the forceful thrust of his erection. Angie trembled as he sealed her to him, and shut her eyes tightly as a wild tide of longing quivered along her weakened length. Her body remembered the hard, sleek heat of his possession and ached intolerably for what it had once known so briefly.

His tongue played an erotic, teasing game with the sensitive interior of her mouth, and she jerked and squirmed against him as if she were being tortured, tiny little pleading cries breaking low in her throat as she clutched at every part of him she could reach, hands sliding beneath his jacket to feel the warmth of his skin through the silk shirt beneath.

Leo lifted his head, dark golden eyes ablaze with primal satisfaction. 'You need this as much as I do...'

With an expert hand he reached beneath her and unclasped her bra, staring intently down at her as he smoothed the straps down her extended arms and tossed the garment out of his way. His smouldering and appreciative gaze swept down, like a kiss of fire, over the full, pouting mounds of breasts crowned by hard rosy nipples, and Angie made a sudden instinctive move to cover herself from that all-encompassing scrutiny. With a ragged laugh, Leo closed both hands over hers and prevented her.

'I ache...I want to ravish every bit of you at once,' Leo confided hungrily. 'But at the same time I want to make you beg because it's better that way—a slow, steady torment all the way to paradise.'

His intense sensuality sent treacherous excitement sweeping over her. She couldn't look away from his eyes any more than she could stop the burning deep down inside her. And, when he bowed his sleek dark head over her bared breasts and allowed the tip of his tongue to flick one taut pink crest, Angie's spine arched up and she gasped and tore her hands free to plunge them into his hair and force him down to her. He curved knowing fingers round the sensitive flesh straining up for his attention, and gently toyed with the aching tips until she thought she might pass out from sheer frustration.

She heard someone moaning, didn't realise it was herself. She couldn't stay still, and she gave a cry of satisfaction as Leo suddenly drove his hands beneath her hips and crushed her beneath him, the carnal force of his mouth devouring hers as he settled himself hungrily between her eagerly spread thighs. The weight and the feel of him against the most sensitive spot in her entire body drove her wild. Unbearable heat pulsed at the very heart of her...until Leo rolled back from her with a low-pitched but splintering curse.

Only then did Angie hear the knocking on the door. Raking smoothing fingers through his black hair, Leo sprang off the bed. Forced back to reality by his desertion, Angie initially froze, and then every nerve switched channel from screaming frustration to appalled shock at her own abandoned behaviour.

'Don't you dare answer that door!' she whispered fiercely in horror as she flew off the bed and intercepted him. 'I don't want anyone to know you've been in here!'

Tugging the door open a couple of inches, keeping her partially clothed body well out of view, Angie popped her head into the gap to say breathlessly, 'Sorry; I was in the bath.'

'Miss Davis asked me to tell you that she would be putting your little boy to bed soon,' an unfamiliar maid in a uniform informed her.

'Thanks. I'll be with her in ten minutes,' Angie promised, assailed by a rollicking tide of maternal guilt as she closed the door again.

Leo strode forward with flaring dark eyes. 'I said that you weren't to be disturbed—'

'What a pity you didn't observe that same courtesy yourself!' Her face was scorched with mortified colour as she looked down at the wanton bareness of her swollen breasts and hurriedly turned a defensive back on him. 'Now, will you please leave? I want nothing more to do with you—'

'Until the next time…and the next time after that,' Leo incised with supreme self-assurance, making her rigid spine notch even tighter with tension. 'Some hungers you can't fight and this is one of them. You're mine now, and you might as well get used to the idea. After all, I can offer you so much.'

That cynicism sliced jagged pain through Angie. 'You're so romantic, Leo.'

'You'd be surprised how romantic I once was.' A soft, derisive laugh punctuated the admission as he opened the door. 'But I grew out of that particular habit. What we have now is basic, honest and much more to my taste.'

'Damn you, we have nothing! Don't you listen to anything I say?' Angie flung almost wildly over her shoulder.

'I'll listen when you start talking sense.' His shrewd gaze scanned her flushed and defensive face. 'I also suggest that after you see Jake you go back to bed and dine off a tray. To be frank, you look lousy.'

Her head was still heavy, her throat raw, but she wasn't prepared to use a common cold as an excuse to avoid the dinner table. Indeed, as she slid in haste into the scoop-necked black body and long turquoise cotton skirt which were the only remotely suitable garments she had to grace such an occasion, she marvelled at Leo's unusually poor advice.

Wallace Neville despised cowardice, and if she failed to put in an appearance he would assume that she had shrunk from the challenge of behaving like a normal guest. Refusing to let herself think of what had almost happened with Leo, Angie dragged a brush through her tangled hair and hurried down the corridor to the nursery suite.

Harriet Davis was reading Jake a story. He was tucked

into a bed with a safety rail attached, drowsy dark eyes already halfway to closing. He livened up briefly at his mother's appearance, and chattered at an incoherent rate of knots about the horses he had seen. Winding down again, he accepted a hug and was asleep within minutes.

'Sorry you were left to hold the fort,' Angie said uncomfortably.

'But that's what I'm here for, Miss Brown,' the older woman responded in some surprise. 'Jake's a joy to look after, too, not a bit shy or strange. You won't need to worry about him while you're downstairs either. I'll be just through there—' she indicated the connecting bedroom '—with the door wide open in case he should wake up.'

Angie tensed as the big Edwardian gong that announced pre-dinner drinks sounded in the distance. 'Jake usually only wakes up if he has a nightmare.'

She started back down the corridor, moving very much more slowly this time. Leo, she thought in sudden tearing pain, without conscience employing her own physical weakness against her like a weapon of destruction. He had no doubt that she would surrender. He had had no doubt two and a half years ago either, and in the space of forty-eight hours he had satisfied his curiosity and his lust and walked away from her again. He had taught her a hard lesson, but she might have handled that rejection better had he been less brutally candid...

'*This*...' Leo had drawled with ice-cold clarity, 'has been a serious error of judgement on my part. Sober and in a more stable state of mind, I would never have taken you to my bed.'

'You wanted me.' Angie had been devastated by the speed with which he had changed towards her. She had slept the night through with a lover and woken up to a stranger.

'*Cristos*...I have had nothing but my own company for months on end! I wanted a woman...I *needed* a woman,'

Leo had spelt out with harsh emphasis. 'And you were in the wrong place at the wrong time.'

Just like an accident waiting to happen, Angie reflected now in growing anguish. What had been true then was no less true now. Unlike Leo, she didn't make serious errors of judgement where matters of the heart were concerned. Nothing so logical had betrayed her...because she wasn't logical about Leo Demetrios. Never had been. Not from the day he had married Petrina and Angie had been physically sick with distress—and certainly not when he had lounged back in the meadow grass two years later in tight, faded jeans and an open-necked shirt, a bottle of Metaxa brandy in one hand and the look of the devil about to reel in a poor lost soul in his smouldering dark eyes...

She had fallen so hard and so heavy, she hadn't known what had hit her, had sunk without trace the minute he'd switched the heat on. Overpowered, overwhelmed, *obsessed*, she conceded fearfully, recoiling. Pale and trembling, she finally reached the ground floor, torn in two already, wanting, *needing* to see Leo again with that part of her she couldn't control, but what brain power she retained frantically urging her to keep her distance and protect herself. She hesitated and then her chin came up and she walked, head held high, into the drawing room.

Leo swung round and she saw only him, the severe tailoring of his dinner jacket accentuating his magnificent physique and spectacular dark good looks. Angie's heart gave a gigantic thud much as if she had just fallen down a ravine. She stilled, wild rose-pink suffusing her cheeks as she met his intensely dark eyes. With a far from steady hand she accepted a glass of sherry from the tray extended by a maid, and Leo curved an arm round Angie's waist, welding her up against a lean hip with an intimacy that was completely unexpected.

'*Angie...?*' a familiar male voice questioned dubiously.

Her startled gaze only then took in the rest of the room,

skimming to the slimly built blond man lodged beside Wallace. And there her attention stayed. She went white. It was Drew, his handsome face revealing his astonishment at her sudden appearance in the family drawing room.

Shock set in hard and fast on Angie. Instantly she registered the danger she was in. While she struggled to conceal her horror, her mind reeled off in fearful, frantic circles. What price Drew's supposed fathering of Jake now? When Drew had made that malicious claim he had undoubtedly assumed that Angie would choose to have an abortion. Drew would have had no thought of his own lies coming back to haunt him. Was he now aware that she had given birth, and that that child was at this very moment sleeping upstairs, acknowledged by both Wallace and Leo as *his* son?

'Someone might have told me that Angie was back.' Drew was rather flushed and stiff, but he managed to laugh.

'Christmas is a time of reconciliation,' Wallace remarked smoothly.

'Dining with us too,' Drew continued tightly. 'Has something changed around here that I should know about?'

'Doubtless Leo has Angie in an arm-lock for some good reason best known to himself.' His grandfather angled a surprisingly amused look of enquiry in their direction.

Angie reddened, and jerked away from Leo as if she had been surprised in an indecent act. Outside the door, the dinner gong sounded again.

Drew was frowning at Angie. 'You're here with Leo?'

Angie uttered a strangled laugh. 'Good heavens, are you kidding? Leo and *me*?' she appealed in an emphatic but distinctly high-pitched denial.

A split second later, she stole an involuntary glance at Leo and then wished she hadn't. Leo gave her a hard-edged smile that chilled her to the marrow and turned her already queasy stomach over sickly.

'Dinner, before the staff get in a fuss,' Wallace decreed,

seemingly oblivious to the strong discordant undertones in the atmosphere.

Drew shot forward and planted himself beside Angie as she moved out of the room. 'What the hell's going on here?' he whispered confidentially out of the side of his mouth.

Angie ignored him, distaste and bitterness suddenly filling her. Drew, who had maligned her to Leo. He might at least have left her with her reputation. As for Leo, why hadn't he at least warned her that Drew was here? And did his cousin's arrival lie behind his firmly delivered suggestion that she remain upstairs for the evening?

Her stomach churned. How soon would the balloon go up on her charade? Unless she was very much mistaken, Drew was the only person present not yet aware of Jake's existence and the lie she had allowed to stand unchallenged.

Dinner was served in the sombre oak-panelled dining room. A manservant pulled out her chair and shook out her napkin. Even in her abstracted state, Angie was disconcerted by the sheer number of new staff in the house, each of them as unfamiliar to her as the maid who had earlier come to her bedroom door. When she'd been here two and a half years ago, her father had served the meals with the aid of the cook's helper. Now he was stationed at the head of the room, frowning loftily in this direction, angling his head in another, silently orchestrating the whole show like some grand master of ceremonies.

While Angie ignored the first course and sank two glasses of wine as she waited for the axe of retribution to fall, Drew dealt her frequent curious glances, but concentrated on talking at length about his career as an advertising executive in New York. He referred on three separate occasions to an award he had won, and energetically pushed the image of himself as a thrusting success story.

Apparently enthralled, Leo asked several encouraging questions which seemed perfectly polite, yet inexplicably

Drew's replies continually made the younger man sound boastful, vain and smug. Wallace merely responded to the flood of information with an occasional distant nod of acknowledgement.

'Of course, I'm presently considering a transfer to London,' Drew informed them all with an expansive smile during the main course. 'I can't tell you how good it feels to be home again, Gramps. I can see there's been a few improvements around here too...'

'Possibly rather more than you can imagine,' his grandfather remarked.

'The old place did need some work. If you like, you can take me round after dinner and show me what you've been doing,' Drew told the old man with the selfless air of one bestowing a generous favour he didn't expect to enjoy.

'I should think you would be very bored,' Leo murmured drily, his strong, dark face hard as iron.

Drew's smile held, but with the suggestion of gritted teeth. 'If there's one thing that living abroad has taught me, it's the importance of valuing my home.'

'I'm afraid it's rather too late for that, Drew,' Wallace said flatly. 'Two years ago, I sold the Court, lock, stock and barrel, to Leo.'

Her eyes dilating in sheer shock, Angie's hand jerked and she almost knocked her wineglass over. Drew gaped at his grandfather in rampant disbelief. A grim smile of satisfaction set Wallace's mouth and it was, Angie sensed, the first genuine emotion the old man had so far revealed. Only Leo was left untouched by the byplay.

CHAPTER SIX

WALLACE NEVILLE cleared his throat with precision, his attention now squarely centred on Drew's shattered face. 'Thanks to your mismanagement, the estate was running at a loss and your debts almost ruined me. The Court needed extensive repairs and I was in no position to finance them. I always believed that I only held this estate in trust for future generations. It will be safe in Leo's hands as it would not have been safe in yours.'

Drew's face went from shocked pallor to furiously flushed during that speech. Angie didn't know where to look and wasn't sure how much more her nerves could take. She too was devastated by the news that Leo now owned Deveraux Court, but she was also feeling grossly uncomfortable sitting in on a discussion of confidential family matters.

'Why didn't you tell me two years ago?' Drew demanded with stark, angry resentment. 'Didn't you think I had the right to know?'

'No,' Wallace said simply. 'When you left me alone to sink or swim with your debts, you lost any right you might have had to have a say in what I did with the Court. But don't worry, Drew...Leo paid a most handsome price, and my personal coffers are full again.'

As Drew recoiled from that unvarnished insult, Angie rose abruptly from her seat. 'I think you'd all be much more comfortable having this conversation in private—'

'Nonsense, girl!' Wallace told her with sharp impatience. 'Sit down and keep quiet. There's more, and it concerns you as well.'

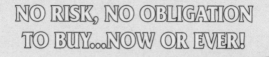

The Harlequin Reader Service®—Here's how it works:

Accepting free books places you under no obligation to buy anything. You may keep the books and gift and return the shipping statement marked "cancel." If you do not cancel, about a month later we'll send you 6 additional novels and bill you just $3.12 each, plus 25¢ delivery per book and applicable sales tax, if any.* That's the complete price — and compared to cover prices of $3.75 each — quite a bargain! You may cancel at any time, but if you choose to continue, every month we'll send you 6 more books, which you may either purchase at the discount price...or return to us and cancel your subscription.

*Terms and prices subject to change without notice. Sales tax applicable in N.Y.

If offer card is missing write to: Harlequin Reader Service, 3010 Walden Ave., P.O. Box 1867, Buffalo NY 14240-1867

BUSINESS REPLY MAIL

FIRST-CLASS MAIL   PERMIT NO. 717   BUFFALO, NY

POSTAGE WILL BE PAID BY ADDRESSEE

HARLEQUIN READER SERVICE
3010 WALDEN AVE
PO BOX 1867
BUFFALO NY 14240-9952

NO POSTAGE
NECESSARY
IF MAILED
IN THE
UNITED STATES

'*Me?*' Angie questioned as she sank reluctantly back down into her chair.

'How can it possibly concern her? And would someone please tell me what she's doing here in the middle of all this?' Drew grated in furious frustration.

'You have a short memory,' Leo breathed very softly.

'*She* is the cat's mother,' Wallace responded with sardonic amusement as he surveyed his bewildered and furious grandson. 'Angie is the mother of your child, Drew. Now isn't that an unexpected Christmas present?'

Angie's facial muscles froze. She was aghast by the announcement.

'The mother of my *what...*?' Drew repeated explosively.

'Angie didn't have that convenient abortion,' Leo supplied very drily. 'She has a son.'

'If she has, he's—' His mouth suddenly snapping shut again like a trap as he evidently recalled his own claim to be the father of her child, Drew shot Angie an incredulous, nakedly accusing glance. 'Bloody hell, what is this?' he demanded rawly as he shot upright and glowered down at his grandfather. 'Some sort of ceremonial witch hunt? Why did you invite me home for Christmas?'

'As long as I'm alive, you'll always be welcome here,' Wallace informed him smoothly. 'But I thought I ought to inform you that you now stand in great danger of being disinherited in favour of your son.'

'*Disinherited...?*' Drew ejaculated wrathfully.

Leo had stiffened. Beneath Angie's shattered gaze, a stark frown drew his black brows together as he studied his grandfather. It was obvious to Angie even in her shaken state that that particular announcement had come as a complete surprise to Leo as well.

Without a word or a further look in anyone's direction, Angie thrust her chair noisily back, rose unsteadily and walked quickly out of the room.

She was so devastated by what had taken place in the

dining room that she was trembling, her head pounding, beads of perspiration dampening her brow as she took instant flight deep into the bowels of the house. She had been right to be suspicious of Wallace's change of heart, she thought strickenly. Outraged by his grandson's desertion, Wallace Neville had set them all up. The old man was trying to use her son as a weapon with which to punish Drew.

And she couldn't let Wallace do that; she couldn't possibly...indeed she ought to be walking back in there right now and telling the lot of them that Jake was Leo's son, not Drew's. But no doubt Drew was already loudly performing that particular task for her, she could not credit that he would remain silent in the face of that final, outrageous threat.

She found herself in the Orangery in the north wing—in its time a favourite schoolgirl haunt of hers because it had never been used by the family. But that vast and once extremely shabby forerunner of the modern day conservatory was barely recognisable to her astonished gaze. The worn mosaic-tiled floor had been restored to perfection. Water now played softly in the bronze lion fountain, and the lush foliage of towering, healthy plants was accentuated by concealed and undoubtedly very expensive lighting. A choked laugh escaped Angie then.

Oh, dear heaven, where had her eyes been since they'd arrived? The unusually pristine order of the grounds, the huge increase in staff, the absence of the smallest speck of dust, the exquisitely presented food and elaborate menu at the dinner table... So many changes, and all of them speaking of infinitely greater wealth than Wallace had ever possessed.

'Angie...?'

Her bowed shoulders jerked up straight again, but she just couldn't make herself turn round and face Leo. But at least she knew that he didn't know he was a father yet, she conceded dully... *How* did she know? That deep, dark drawl had been too quiet and too controlled.

Predictably, Leo strode right into her view path to challenge her evasion. His heartbreakingly handsome features had a hard, forbidding cast that instantly disturbed her and she tore her eyes swiftly from him again.

'I wasn't aware that Wallace had invited Drew. He didn't tell me,' Leo admitted harshly. 'Nor had I any idea what his plans were. I would not have knowingly brought you into a situation like this.'

'My father works for you now,' Angie whispered shakily.

Light and shadow played across the sculpted angles of Leo's strong face, his lean, hard body poised in predatory masculine stillness. He allowed the silence to gather and lie.

Angie shivered, skin clammy, head beginning to swim. She spun violently away. 'Damn you, Leo,' she said chokily. 'You should've told me!'

'It wasn't relevant—'

'Not relevant?' she echoed unevenly, thinking that only a male as immensely wealthy as Leo could dismiss the purchase of an ancestral home, an estate which ran to several thousand acres and a whole village full of tenants with such careless cool.

'Wallace now occupies a suite of rooms on the ground floor, but only because he was finding the stairs a challenge. To all intents and purposes, he is as much master here as he ever was, and I would not have it any other way,' Leo told her curtly. 'Drew almost bankrupted him. I bought because I had to buy, *not* out of any desire to deprive Drew of what he always fondly believed would be his.'

Angie was finding it very hard to concentrate. 'He would've sold it anyway,' she muttered, speaking the thought out loud without meaning to.

The silence came back, thunderous as a storm warning.

'It's been an educational evening,' Leo finally murmured darkly, striking off on a conversational tangent just as she had minutes earlier, and in so doing revealing that on some deep, atavistic level below that surface composure Leo was infinitely more tense than he appeared.

Angie curved her arms round her trembling body, aching just at the sound of his voice. 'Terrifying,' she whispered in stark truth.

'Look at me...' Leo urged harshly.

'I *can't*...' How was she ever going to meet his eyes while she told him? Told him that her son was also his son? He would hit the roof. He would hate her. He wouldn't turn his back and walk away from Jake. No, he would accept the burden of responsibility, but despise her utterly for putting him in that position.

'*Cristos!*' Leo grated with explosive abruptness as he settled a powerful hand on her shoulder and flipped her round to face him. 'I said, look at me!'

Shivering and unsteady on her feet, she staggered slightly until he steadied her. She stared up at him, mouth dry, heart hammering like a wild thing in terror inside her breast. He searched her huge, shadowed eyes, the feverish flush demarcating her taut cheekbones, and just as suddenly set her back from him in a move of open, outright repulsion, his bold, dark features clenching with fierce derision.

Without warning, Leo attacked. 'You little bitch...you couldn't take your eyes off him!'

The onslaught of that black, murderous fury shook Angie inside out with shock. 'No—I—'

Leo spread his arms in an all-encompassing and violent gesture of disgust and dropped them again, glittering dark eyes raking over her quailing figure. 'He bedded you, he knocked you up and then he dumped you. *Theos*...not content with that, he bragged about his so-macho behaviour! And yet tonight he walked in after over two years and all of a sudden there was nobody else in that room for you *but* him!'

Angie was feeling horribly dizzy. 'It w-wasn't like that—'

'Perhaps you didn't note his reaction to the news that you had had the baby,' Leo derided with blistering effect. 'He'd forgotten that there was ever a problem, and he was appalled. If he hadn't remembered just in time that he had boasted about his virility, he would've denied all responsibility!'

Angie pressed a weak hand to her throbbing brow. 'Leo…I have something to tell you—'

'No, you have nothing to tell me and nothing I could want to hear,' Leo interrupted with ruthless finality as he scanned her distraught face. 'What I wanted to know I learnt at first hand tonight. You're still besotted with Drew.'

'I'm not besot—'

'You're pathetic, Angie!' Leo gritted half under his breath as he slung her one last hard, punishing glance then strode away.

'Leo!' she gasped strickenly, moving after him, and then freezing into mortified paralysis as Drew appeared in the doorway.

'She's all yours!' Leo drawled with crushing clarity as he brushed past his cousin.

Feeling as weak as a half-drowned kitten, Angie made it over to one of the capacious basketwork armchairs and fell down into it before her wobbling legs folded beneath her.

'What's got into him?' Drew enquired irritably as he came to a halt several feet away.

'Your filthy lies,' Angie informed him with a convulsive swallow.

Drew stiffened. 'So Leo told you…'

'Yes.'

'Well, we all get a little foolish when we've had a few drinks too many,' Drew said in insultingly casual acknowledgement and dismissal of what he had done. 'But that still doesn't explain why everyone is running round with the idea that your brat is mine! Why didn't *you* tell Wallace and Leo the truth?'

Angie buried her aching head in her hands. 'I'm not feeling well enough for this.'

'Too bad…you've made a real hash of my home-coming!' he condemned.

'You did a hateful thing, Drew…don't try to put all the blame for this situation on me,' Angie warned him heavily.

Silence stretched for several taut seconds.

'It's very easily sorted,' Drew told her with studied casualness then. 'You just tell Leo that when you first became pregnant you assumed that the baby was mine, and then later realised your mistake.'

A hoarse laugh was dredged from Angie. Same old Drew, she noted dully. Drew had always been enormously, ridiculously conscious of his image where Leo was concerned. He didn't want to be branded a boastful liar. He didn't want it known even now that they had *never* been lovers! Disgusted by his selfishness, Angie forced her hands down on the chair arms and raised herself up again.

'Where are you going?'

'Bed… I'll tell Leo the truth when you tell him the truth,' Angie asserted unsteadily, but the look in her feverish blue eyes was one of fierce, immovable conviction.

Drew looked angrily incredulous at the challenge. 'He wouldn't believe me!'

'Then you'll have to work at being convincing…because I will not pretend that I was a promiscuous slut to promote your Mr Cool image!'

'My God…what do you have to lose? *Leo?* You never could catch him to keep, but that kid of yours could be your meal ticket for life! So why hold off on breaking the glad tidings?'

Appalled by a viciousness that Drew had never aimed at

her before, Angie stared back at him with pained incomprehension.

'OK...so Leo isn't likely to greet a little bastard with joy,' Drew conceded with a twist of his lips. 'Particularly not when he's already got Marisa Laurence lined up as Mrs Demetrios number two. But I should think he'll make it well worth your while to keep a low profile, and you'll certainly never have to hire yourself out as an au pair again.'

Angie had turned bone-white. A trickle of perspiration ran down between her heaving breasts as she dragged in a tremulously short and inadequate breath to sustain herself. 'Marisa...Laurence?'

Drew elevated a knowing brow, cruel amusement in his gaze as he scanned her stricken pallor. 'He's known her practically all his life,' he reminded her unnecessarily. 'Whatever recent spoke you contrived to put in the wheel of their relationship would seem to me to have snapped tonight...and Marisa is a very determined lady. If I were you, I'd settle for what I could get off Leo fast!'

Briefly, Angie closed her aching eyes, and then she began to walk away, afraid she would collapse where she stood if she didn't stay on the move. Marisa Laurence...daughter of the only other major landowner in the area and, even in Angie's time, a regular visitor to the Court. An elegant, dainty blonde, who had always made Angie feel like a great, hulking amazon. An ocean of pain filled her to overflowing and it was almost more than she could bear. So *that* was who Leo had been with the night before he flew to Brussels!

'Tell me one thing...' she whispered tautly without turning her head again. 'What changed you from a friend I trusted into an enemy?'

Drew gave her a sullen look. 'You've finally noticed, have you? Haven't you worked it out yet?' he prompted thinly. 'Two and a half years ago, I was in love with you!'

Stunned, Angie jerked as if he had struck her. 'No...'

'Oh, yes,' Drew countered, with a bitter edge to the assurance that was horribly persuasive. 'I wasn't too proud to take on my lofty cousin's left-overs but, unfortunately, Leo didn't leave much of you intact, did he? You were like a walking, talking shell with nobody home inside. You just used me to save face with Leo!'

Angie felt sick to her stomach with shame. It was true. In a sense, she had. She had been every bit as obsessed with her own agony as he accused her of being, wholly blind, it seemed, to what was happening right under her own nose.

'I'm sorry, Drew...I really am,' she managed through the thickness of tears clogging her throat as she forced herself back round to look at him.

'Forget it. If you hadn't been pregnant by him, I might have persuaded you to marry me.' Drew grimaced as he drew level with her. 'And what a huge mistake that would have been! No, don't bother to apologise...if you'd married me, I would've had to lock you up and throw away the key every time Leo came to visit. You've been his so long I don't think you could ever learn to be anyone else's.'

'It's not like that any more!' she protested instantaneously.

'Isn't it?' Drew studied her ashen colour and bruised eyes with a superior smile that savaged her already battered ego. 'All you've got left now is your pride, Angie. That's the real reason why you don't want to tell Leo that he's the father of your son. And even I have sympathy for what you've got ahead of you. Scratch an inch beneath Leo's tough hide and you'll uncover the rigid moral values of a far from swinging dinosaur. An illegitimate son will hit his ego where it really hurts, and he is one of the most unforgiving bastards I've ever come across!'

As Drew strode off down the corridor, Angie steadied

herself on the door handle and then pressed her burning brow against the cold glass pane.

A careful arm drew her back. 'You should be in bed...you're running one of those crazy temperatures you always run when you catch a cold.'

Woozily, Angie focused on her father's concerned face. 'Dad?' she said, frowning with disconcertion.

'I like to keep my personal life private,' Samuel Brown admitted stiffly as he supported her uncertain steps down the dimly lit corridor. 'It's been over two years, Angie. I didn't want to greet my daughter and meet my grandson for the first time in front of my employer. It wasn't the time or the place. But you're still my daughter, and nothing can change that.'

Tears drenched her already strained eyes. 'I thought you were so a-angry with me...'

'We all make mistakes, Angie. Me...you,' he responded stiltedly. 'Perhaps if you'd talked to me before you ran away I could have helped.'

Briefly, she angled her head down awkwardly on his shoulder. It was difficult. He was so much smaller than she was, but it was the closest she dared come to giving him a grateful hug. He was not a demonstrative man and emotional displays embarrassed him. Possibly that more than anything else had served to keep them in their separate corners when she'd first arrived in his life as a grieving and undeniably resentful teenager. Yet now she sensed the alteration in him, the softening of his rigid outlook and values, and absently wondered what on earth could have brought about such a change at his time in life.

'I'll send Emily up, shall I?' he offered as they reached the top of the service staircase he had used as a short cut. 'She could help you into bed.'

Angie stiffened and drew away from her father into the bedroom corridor. 'No...don't bother Em; I'll be fine now.

Goodnight, Dad...and thanks,' she completed, almost as stilted in her careful restraint as he was.

Her head was spinning round and round. She felt nauseous and cold and horribly dizzy. She trailed a hand along the wall as a guide, and then that hand became a necessary brace to keep herself upright as she stopped, dimly registered the sound of hurrying footsteps, and turned her swimming head.

Leo seemed to be striding towards her in slow motion. She swayed and then a pair of hands caught her as she began to slide inexorably down. But it was Leo who snatched her up into his arms, Leo whom she saw last before the blackness folded in, and Leo whom she heard say grimly, 'All right, Brown...I'll deal with this.'

'Angie wouldn't thank you for calling a doctor, sir,' Samuel Brown was saying in his most distant voice when Angie surfaced in what felt like a delirious dream. 'She hates a fuss being made, and she'll probably be right as rain by the morning—'

'Probably?' Leo interrupted, sounding exasperated. 'She could have pneumonia—'

'I don't think so, sir. The first time she ran a temperature like that, she gave us quite a fright too, but it's just the way she is. Please don't concern yourself. Emily's got her into bed now, and she'll stay with her tonight—'

'I said I would...do I need a chaperon?' Leo enquired grittily.

'Mr Wallace once said that my daughter needed a full-time bodyguard in this household. In my capacity as a parent, I agreed with the concern he expressed, sir.'

In the electric silence which followed, Angie focused hazily on Leo. His hard, classic profile had all the yielding qualities of granite. She sensed his outrage, and marvelled at her father's comeback.

'I was concerned about her,' Leo breathed tautly.

'Most kind of you, sir…but there's really no need for you to disturb yourself.'

No, no need at all for him to disturb himself, Angie thought wretchedly. If Drew was right, Leo already had another far more suitable woman in his life. Angie drifted away again into an uneasy slumber.

The next time her eyes opened, her head no longer swam and she felt infinitely more normal, but she was desperately thirsty. Daylight was filtering through a gap in the curtains, outlining the dark shapes of the furniture and framing the male poised by the tall window. Leo, immaculate in a fabulous silver-grey suit worn with a pale shirt and dark tie. As she began to sit up, he swung fluidly round and looked right at her.

Her heart slammed against her breastbone so hard, she couldn't breathe. Those brilliant dark eyes of his, full of such restive energy and such fierce strength of will. Those eyes pierced her like a hot knife sinking into honey, made her burn and ache and crave…made her so very, very weak. And she knew then—could no longer lie to herself—that she still loved Leo. Drew's sharp tongue had penetrated her defences and forced her to accept that truth. No cure, just endure, she reflected painfully.

'I found your stepmother asleep in the chair in the early hours. I sent her to bed.'

Angie had a dim recollection of Emily fussing round her at some stage of the night, silently offering her a refreshing drink and then retreating as fast as she possibly could back into the shadows. Both of them felt uncomfortable with each other now. That was hardly surprising after what had happened, but Angie knew that she would need to seal that breach with her stepmother if she didn't want her father to notice that there was something wrong.

'I'm heading back to London for a couple of days tomorrow,' Leo continued without any expression at all.

Heart and hope hit the floor with a resounding crash and

she hated herself, snatching at the glass of water by the bed with a clumsy hand, cupping the cold tumbler between spread fingers and sipping with all the finesse of a toddler at a plastic cup.

'Drew's girlfriend, Tally, will be arriving soon…'

Tell him he's Jake's father; get it over with, common sense urged. Why bother? Why cause all that trouble? a little voice enquired more seductively. Tell Wallace, let the old man do what he will with that news and then leave while Leo is away. Her father would loan her some money to get by on…

'So I suggest that you return to London with me,' Leo completed quietly.

'No!' Her tortured eyes flew back to him in reproach.

Leo vented a soft, chilling laugh. 'Not to share my bed, or even to share the same roof. I did assume that I'd been sufficiently frank last night, but apparently not. I've withdrawn from the fray, Angie… But I *was* responsible for bringing you here and I don't think it's a very good idea for you to remain.'

A tide of unbearable pain engulfed Angie. 'So I'm being thrown out.'

'Rescued, saved from yourself,' Leo contradicted her drily. 'Do I really need to spell it out? You, Jake, Drew and his girlfriend round the same table… Currently, Wallace appears to be remarkably indifferent to everything but his own overweening desire to make Drew sweat blood. At heart, however, he's still fond of my cousin, and, while he may well make provision for Jake in his will, I seriously doubt that Drew will lose much by it.'

Those thefts, those wretched, ghastly thefts, she reflected in anguished resentment. Naturally, Leo believed that she would hang around like the spectre at the feast if there was any prospect of eventual profit. And the truth would never come out now; how could it? Emily would take her guilty secret to the grave with her and, for her father's sake, Angie had urged that secrecy on her terrified stepmother.

She turned very pale. 'You think that money really matters to me, don't you?'

Leo studied her with glittering dark eyes, his high cheekbones and his faintly blue-shadowed jaw taut and hard as steel. 'I think you're dangerous, and that as my mistress you would be even more dangerous and quite capable of tearing this family apart.'

'I won't *be* your mistress…there was never any chance of that!' Angie swore on the back of an angry sob.

A black brow rose in arrogant disagreement. 'Wasn't there? But that's immaterial now. I still refuse to stand back on the sidelines and watch you with Drew.'

A phone buzzed, preternaturally loud in the oppressive silence. Leo dug a portable out of his pocket, frowned and strode to the door. 'I'll see you later,' he told her flatly.

'Leo…!' Angie called after him in frustration.

But the door closed and, just as suddenly, Angie had had enough of her charade. As soon as she was dressed, she would face Leo and get it over with. With that decision made, she scrambled out of bed, ran herself a bath, decided that her hair simply had to be washed and finally emerged to pull on a straight denim skirt and her favourite black sweater. Only while she was drying her hair did she realise that she had slept in and that it was already almost ten in the morning.

The nursery was empty, both Jake and his nanny absent. Angie descended the stairs and, espying her father in the hall below, leant over to ask, 'Where's Jake?'

'Out on a walk with Harriet and the dog.'

'Leo…?'

'Business. He's gone for the day, I should think.'

Angie groaned. She should have thought of that, shouldn't have baulked at racing down the corridor after him in her nightie and bare feet. 'Do you have the number of his mobile phone?' she asked abruptly.

Her father went poker-faced as if he had been asked for the crown jewels.

'Dad, don't be silly.'

In possession of the number, Angie went into the study to use the extension there.

'Demetrios,' Leo answered impatiently, and she could hear male voices talking somewhere in the background.

'It's Angie…' She sucked in a deep, audible breath. 'I've been thinking and…I really do need to talk to you.'

'This is not the most convenient moment,' Leo responded coolly. 'What is it?'

'Leo, this isn't something I could discuss on the phone…it's something very…well, very—'

'Very, very *what*?'

'Private, personal…' Angie almost whispered, twisting the phone cord round and round her restive fingers. 'It concerns you and…er…me.'

The silence on the line thundered.

'*Really…?*' Leo breathed very low, his deep, dark drawl roughening to send a curious buzz down her tense spinal cord.

'I just wanted to be sure of seeing you alone as soon as you get back. I thought we could meet in the Orangery.'

'Make it my private suite. The Orangery struck me as distinctly over-populated last night.'

'When?' Angie muttered tautly.

'I'll use the helicopter…expect me within the hour,' Leo murmured huskily, and then she heard him say quite distinctly, 'Gentlemen, this meeting is dismissed,' before he cut the connection.

Within the hour? That *was* a surprise, but a very welcome one. She would feel much better once this confrontation with Leo was over, she told herself staunchly. She was incredibly grateful that he had evidently recognised her anxiety and grasped that she had something very important to tell him.

As Wallace rarely made a public appearance before noon and Drew had never been an early riser, Angie breakfasted alone in the cosy morning room where she flipped nervously through the newspapers and drank coffee like a caffeine addict. She wondered about Marisa Laurence and resisted the temptation to try and pump her father for information. That sort of request would put him in an awkward position and he would resent it. And, very probably, Drew had only named Marisa out of pure malice. Leo could not be heavily involved with the other woman, she decided.

When Jake came surging in to see her, Angie swept him up in a fierce hug. Twenty minutes later, her father put his head round the door to ask if he could take Jake downstairs to meet the staff.

Both surprised and touched by the request, Angie watched her father and her son walk off hand in hand, and marvelled that her parent had not yet asked her a single awkward question. But then perhaps he judged it wisest not to probe too soon. And he would not be labouring under any misapprehension regarding his grandson's paternity. Angie's cheeks warmed. There had been the most almighty, earth-shattering row when her father had discovered that she'd spent two nights down at the Folly with Leo while he'd been in London with Wallace, staying at the Neville apartment.

Leo's stated hour was almost up. She went upstairs, heading for the Long Gallery where Leo had had his own suite for years. Vibrant Minton majolica ware was displayed in the ornate plaster alcoves. Regency gilt and ebony sofas covered in lemon moire sat at regular intervals below the endless stretch of the mullioned windows. The walls opposite were closely hung with huge family portraits, below which marched an imposing line of marble busts on plinths.

When Angie heard the distant whine of a helicopter, she quickened her steps and in a nerve-racked surge hurried through the main door off the gallery into a part of the house which had until now been forbidden to her. Her father had always held that the family's private rooms were sacrosanct, and she had never dared to take a peek without permission.

She found herself in a very spacious and rather grand sitting room, full of breathtaking early oak furniture and wonderfully comfortable-looking settees and armchairs. According to her father, through the door on the left lay a bedroom, dressing room and bathroom, and through the door on the right lay a room Leo used as an office. She wanted to steal a look beyond both doors, but was terrified of being caught in the act like a nosy schoolgirl.

In fact, terror pretty much encapsulated her entire frame of mind, Angie acknowledged, shamefaced. Leo was so logical, so brutally candid. To ask Leo to understand why she had allowed such a misapprehension to stand…well, it was the equivalent of asking Leo to comprehend madness when he himself was sane.

There was no forewarning of his arrival. The walls were too solid for that. Angie was fiddling with her hair and smoothing down her skirt with moist palms for about the forty-eighth time when the door jerked open. She flinched. Leo thrust it shut behind him with a lean hip while giving Angie the most dazzling smile of raw amusement. That was all she saw—that fantastic smile flashing across his darkly handsome features like blinding sunshine on a wintry day. It transfixed her to the spot, every pulse in her body going crazy in tune to her racing heartbeat.

But then Leo broke the spell of his own enchantment by suddenly tossing the most enormous bouquet of red roses into her startled arms. Wide-eyed and wildly taken aback by that unforeseen development, Angie only just managed to catch them, and only then noticed the silver ice bucket he had had tucked under one arm and which he was now setting down. While Angie watched in sheer, wordless paralysis, Leo withdrew two glasses from a cabinet, popped the cork on the champagne with a noise as loud as a pistol crack and sent the contents foaming expertly down into the waiting glasses.

'Do you know I've never bought flowers for a woman before? I guess you might have worked that out for yourself when I threw them at you,' he murmured with wry self-mockery. 'My father always said that the giving of flowers was irredeemably wet, the sole exception to the rule being illness or burial.'

Angie's throat closed over as if a giant hand had squeezed all the life from her vocal cords.

'We'll dine out tonight,' Leo promised, smouldering dark eyes raking over her slender figure in an explicit look of possession. 'This was the best I could do at such short notice, and I have to confess that I'm beginning to feel like a randy teenager trying to slyly seduce a daughter under her father's roof. I will feel much more relaxed about this relationship in London...'

Roses and champagne, Angie reflected, struck dumb by astonishment, her concentration utterly shot by Leo's blazing good humour and the sinking, sick awareness that somewhere along the line—most probably on the phone line—one of them had got their wires very, very badly crossed...

CHAPTER SEVEN

ANGIE clasped the glass Leo extended, took a deep swig of champagne to moisten her bone-dry mouth and in excruciating discomfiture muttered, 'The roses are just beautiful, *really* they are...but I'm afraid you don't understand why—'

'I understand perfectly.' Helpfully, Leo removed the bouquet she was clutching awkwardly beneath one arm, unbuttoned his well-cut jacket and shrugged indolently free of it. 'You've made the logical choice.' He sipped his champagne, loosened his tie and discarded it one-handed beneath her arrested gaze. 'There's no room for you now in Drew's life. At worst, you'd be an embarrassment, at best a temptation he can ill afford. Tally Richardson is his boss's daughter and he's in deep—'

'That's not what I m-meant, Leo,' Angie interposed in a voice that wobbled in spite of her desperate efforts to keep it steady.

A lean brown hand smoothly detached the glass from her convulsive grip, set it aside with his own. 'Don't be embarrassed, Angie. We won't ever need to discuss Drew again because I won't bring you to the Court when he's visiting Wallace.'

The tip of her tongue snaked out to lick along her lower lip in a frantic, flickering motion, every inch of her whip-taut with tension. 'But you've got the wrong idea... When I phoned you, I wasn't—'

'You're talking too much, *pethi mou*...' His slumbrous gaze appeared to be welded to the soft pink fullness of her mouth and she ran out of breath completely, her breasts tingling in awareness, a shaft of heat feathering between

her trembling thighs. In one slow, powerful movement, Leo
reached out and tugged her into his arms. 'And I am not
in the mood to talk right now...what I want is to lay you
down on my bed and take you over and over again. Then
I will know that there will be *no* going back,' he completed
with ragged emphasis.

His hungry mouth plunged down onto hers in a devour-
ingly passionate kiss that almost brought Angie to her
knees. As he let his tongue slide deep between her lips in
electrifying mimicry of the possession he fully intended to
take place, and she felt the hard, restive probe of his arousal
pressing against her stomach, Angie was clutched by such
a driving, desperate longing to let him do exactly what he
liked with her quivering and all too willing body that she
gave a muffled moan of agonised self-loathing.

With an unashamed growl of hunger, Leo bent and swept
her right off her feet. As he shouldered his sure passage
into the bedroom beyond, Angie was seeing whirling lights
and beckoning paradise. Her fingers speared caressingly
into his thick black hair, palm resting lovingly against one
hard cheekbone. She pressed her reddened lips helplessly
onto the smooth brown skin below his shirt collar and
slowly inhaled the hot, musky scent of him, and then, with
an aching shudder of regret, she gasped, 'Leo...put me
down...*please*!'

He settled her down onto the oak four-poster bed. Whip-
ping her legs below her and sitting up on her knees, Angie
steadied herself on one of the heavily carved, bulbous posts,
guilty blue eyes flying to him as she pushed her tumbled
hair off her brow with a shaking hand. 'You misunderstood
me on the phone...'

In the act of moving towards her, Leo stopped dead.
Ebony brows drawing together, he scanned the pale, tense
triangle of her face. 'What could I possibly have misunderstood? Something very private and personal concerning you
and me; what else is there but *this*?'

Angie gulped. 'It's my fault. How could you know what else there was before I told you?'

'What the hell are you talking about?'

'You'll be very angry—'

'I'm already angry,' Leo countered without a second of hesitation. 'You switch on, you switch off—'

'This isn't about sex. It's about something much more important—'

'At this moment *nothing* could be more important!' Leo delivered with an unashamed snarl of all-male frustration, glittering dark eyes communicating his outrage.

'Leo... Oh, hell, there is just no way to work up to this,' Angie confessed in desperation as she forced herself to meet that fulminating stare. 'Jake is not Drew's son...Jake is yours.'

The silence held...and held long beyond her expectations. She snatched in a shivering breath. Leo was so still, she might not have spoken. And then his bold, dark features clenched in fierce condemnation. 'What kind of a sick joke is that?'

Angie flinched. Tears of stress were building up to burn behind her eyes. 'Ask Drew if you don't believe me,' she advised hoarsely. 'Before I left, I *told* Drew that I was expecting your baby, and, however much of the truth he might choose to give you, he will at least admit that!'

'This is outrageous...' Leo glowered at her in disbelief. 'Drew told me—'

Without warning, temper sparked out of control inside Angie. 'I don't give a hoot what Drew blasted well told you!' she flung at him in a surge of angry humiliation. 'I don't have to make excuses or try to explain away your cousin's stupid, crude lies about me because I had nothing to do with any of that...I wasn't even here!'

Leo had turned very pale beneath his naturally dark skin tone. 'You are lying...you *have* to be—'

'Why must I be lying?' Angie broke in, her voice rising

even more steeply in pitch. 'Because you don't like what you're hearing? Well, that's fine by me, Leo...just you go ahead and tell yourself I'm lying and ignore this whole conversation if—'

'Keep quiet!' Leo thundered back at her.

Angie jerked, lashes fluttering in shock.

'Why are you raving at me like a hysteric?' Leo shot at her in wrathful reproof. '*Theos*...you think any man would just swallow a story like this when you throw it at him out of the blue? I slept with you two and a half years ago. If you were pregnant, you had ample opportunity to tell me then.'

'I didn't want to.'

'And what sort of sense does that make?' His scorching dark eyes were still raw with incredulity. 'Will you listen to yourself?'

Angie lowered her head, intense mortification engulfing her. 'I'm sorry that he is yours, I really am but it's not something I can change. Leo,' she muttered in a driven, unsteady plea, 'what do you see when you look at Jake? He has dark brown eyes, black hair and olive skin—'

'You said that he'd inherited your mother's colouring.'

'I lied. My mother was as fair as I am,' Angie mumbled wretchedly.

'You ran around with Drew and his far from clean-living crowd for many weeks, and half the time he was too drunk to know *what* you were doing!' Leo spelt out with grim emphasis. 'You think I'm fool enough to be impressed by a child's black hair and brown eyes? Who knows who else you might have slept with during that period?'

Angie's stomach clenched. 'I think you've said enough.' She unfolded her legs and slid down off the bed, her lower limbs feeling horribly uncoordinated and clumsy. 'I don't have to take that sort of abuse from anybody.'

Leo closed a lean hand round her forearm before she could sidestep him. 'I'm not about to apologise for saying out loud what any man might think. That's the way I'm made,' he bit out.

Angie was shaking like a leaf in his hold, but her tear-filled eyes blazed with bitter censure. 'You were the first man I ever slept with…on what grounds do you base your suspicion that I turned into a tart within weeks of being with you?'

A dark rise of blood fired over the hard slant of Leo's cheekbones.

'Jake was born eight months and three weeks after that weekend. I have a birth certificate to prove it. He couldn't possibly be anyone else's child.'

'But we didn't have unprotected sex.'

'How do you know?' Angie muttered in reluctant challenge of that point, tension suddenly rocketing sky-high within her again.

Leo stared down at her, spiky black lashes low on his piercing dark eyes. 'You *said* you were on the contraceptive pill. Are you saying that it failed?'

Angie dragged in a slow, shivering breath. 'No…'

'Then what are you saying?' Leo enquired intently.

'I was never on the pill,' Angie said shakily, but she was determined to tell the entire truth. 'I lied about that too.'

'You lied…?' Leo echoed not quite steadily as his hand dropped away from her arm.

Angie tore her shamed gaze from his, face scarlet with guilt, heartbeat banging somewhere in the region of her aching throat, and finally nodded in acknowledgement.

'*Why?*' Leo pressed.

Immense weariness flooded Angie. 'I wanted to get pregnant.'

'You *wanted* to get pregnant?' Leo repeated in an accented drawl thick with incredulity. He prowled restively away from her like a panther pacing a too small cage, only to swing back again within seconds. 'You are openly admitting that to me?'

'Not much point in lying about it now. So you see it's OK to hate me,' Angie conceded chokily.

But Leo wasn't looking at her any more, and a flood of guttural Greek suddenly erupted from him. Before Angie could even catch her breath, Leo strode out of the bedroom at speed, crossed the sitting room beyond and hauled the door onto the Long Gallery open with such raw, physical force that it went slamming back against the wall with a thunderous crash.

'Leo!' Angie cried, chasing after him. 'Where are you going?'

Pure rage blazed from Leo's aggressively set features as he spread both incredibly expressive hands in a violent arc. 'Where do you think?' he slung at her from between clenched white teeth. 'I'm going to rip Drew apart...I want to slam him up against the nearest wall and beat him into a pulp for lying to me!'

In panic, Angie grabbed his arm. 'Leo, *no*!'

Leo shook her off his sleeve and powered on down the gallery with long, purposeful strides. 'I don't care what you did to him...I don't care how infatuated he was...I don't even care that you may well have tried to pass off my child as his to hang onto him!' he vented in a soaring, savage crescendo as he stopped dead to stare back at her where she stood several feet away.

He moved his eloquent hands in raw rebuttal. 'None of that matters. None of that matters a damn,' he framed hoarsely. 'But nothing could ever excuse his lies when my child was at risk... He let you leave this house alone, penniless, and he knew...that sick, selfish, destructive little bastard *knew* that you were carrying my baby, and not only did he not tell me, but he did everything he could to make *sure* that I would have no reason to follow you!'

'Leo...I did not try to pass off my baby as Drew's when I found out I was pregnant,' Angie protested painfully.

'Even if I'd been that kind of woman, I couldn't have because Drew and I were never—'

'*Cristos*...if you hadn't shared yourself between two men in the same family, none of this would ever have happened!' Leo condemned in an onslaught of scorching derision that cut through her like a whip. 'You played us off one against the other and this is the end result!'

'That's not fair,' Angie gasped strickenly. 'I never slept with Drew!'

'I tell you what is not fair,' Leo responded wrathfully, seeming to ignore that claim, and if possible his dark eyes blistered over her distraught face with even greater contempt and condemnation. 'What is not fair is what *you* have done to my son...of all of us the only innocent victim involved!'

Every remaining scrap of colour drained from Angie's cheeks and she fell back from him. Like a juggernaut on automatic pilot, Leo powered on towards the main staircase. But Angie was no longer so keen to race after him and save Drew from certain death. She hadn't played Drew and Leo off one against the other...that was an appalling thing to accuse her of! She had been in too much distress over losing Leo and then discovering that she was pregnant to suspect that Drew cherished far from platonic feelings for her.

An angry shout rudely penetrated her fierce preoccupation, and, with a stifled moan, Angie raced for the stairs, got halfway down them and then froze. Down below in the Great Hall Drew had clearly emerged in all innocence from the morning room, but now he was in definite and hasty retreat. Leo was striding towards him, his dark features set in a mask of savage threat.

'Do I have to chase you to get you to fight?' Leo flung at him with sizzling scorn.

'So Angie finally told you... What's the matter with you?' Drew demanded weakly. 'I did you a favour with that story of mine…and if you'd left well enough alone she'd never have shown her face here again!'

Leo hit Drew with such speed and force that all Angie saw was a blur of motion and then Drew struggling to pick himself up from the floor. Pale as milk and trembling, Angie braced herself on the bannister, her stomach churning.

'Why are you trying to blame me for the fact that you've landed your embarrassing little mistake back on your own doorstep?' Drew spat resentfully.

Just as Leo raked back at him in Greek, the green baize door at the back of the hall swung noisily open and catapulted Jake into the proceedings. With a squeal of pleasure, Jake hurtled across the floor and flung himself in high excitement at Leo's legs. Drew took swift advantage of that unexpected stay of execution and headed fast towards the front door.

'I'm off to the airport to pick up Tally…we'll use the town apartment for a night or two,' Drew flung rather nasally over his shoulder.

Leo said nothing. He didn't even look in his cousin's direction. He was staring fixedly down at Jake, his chiselled profile taut and drawn with strain. Impervious to the atmosphere, the toddler continued to bounce impatiently round his feet, holding his arms up high to be lifted. 'Carry, Leo…carry!' he urged pleadingly.

As Angie's eyes flooded with moisture, man and child swam out of focus. She twisted her head away, fighting to get a grip on her emotions. When she looked again, Leo was crouched down at Jake's level, talking to him. She could see the electric tension in his broad shoulders but she couldn't see his face. As she reached the foot of the stairs, Leo leant forward, scooped his chattering son up into his arms and sprang up again.

He moved with fluid grace in a slow circle as he held Jake high and studied him with fierce, unashamed emo tional intensity. A revealing glitter made his lustrous dark eyes seem more brilliant than ever. Angie's throat closed over. And then he saw her over his son's shoulder and he went rigid, shooting her a look of such volatile and angry condemnation that her stomach muscles contracted as if he had thrown her a punch as well.

'I'm sorry...' she said thickly, overwhelmed by guilt.

'You couldn't ever be sorry enough to satisfy me,' Leo swore with a bitter curve to his eloquent mouth.

Angie made no attempt to follow him as he carried Jake upstairs. In the mood Leo was in, she knew she couldn't handle him, knew that, while she was completely drained, Leo might well warm up for another attack if she put herself in his path again. And he had the right to some time alone with Jake.

'He'll cool off...eventually,' Wallace commented from behind her, making her jump. 'I should give him a very wide berth, though, until he does.'

Angie spun round. Leo's grandfather was already returning to the drawing room. 'It's cold out here. Close the door behind you.'

After a second's pause, Angie recognised the unspoken invitation and followed him. 'You *knew*...?'

'I suspected it long before you even arrived,' the old man confirmed. 'But I knew beyond all reasonable doubt the instant I laid eyes on the little chap.'

'But you...you told Drew...*here* only last night that I was the mother of his child!'

Wallace lowered himself carefully down into an armchair. 'He deserved a good fright. When he lied to Leo, he behaved despicably.' His faded blue eyes rested on Angie's bemused face. 'And if you hadn't told Leo the truth I would've told him for you. If he's like an angry bear now, you have only yourself to thank. You should've known what that little boy would mean to him.'

That rebuke inflamed Angie. 'Not so long ago, you didn't even want me to *have* that child!'

'No, I didn't,' Wallace agreed grimly. 'Not when I was suffering from the mistaken belief that Drew had fathered him. Drew never could measure up to Leo, and the last thing he needed was a wife who had only turned to him because she couldn't have his cousin!'

Angie reddened fiercely. 'I only ever looked on Drew as a friend.'

'And, at the time, I hadn't the foggiest idea that you and Leo had been up to no good down at the Folly,' Wallace admitted with blatant disapproval. 'You'd been keeping company with Drew for weeks. Naturally I assumed that he was responsible for your condition, but I didn't face him with it.'

Angie shifted uncomfortably from one foot to the other, defiance squashed by Wallace's mortifying frankness. She waited in an agony of tension for him to refer to the thefts. Naturally his conviction that she was the household thief had heavily influenced his attitude towards her then as well.

'Then Leo let drop that Drew was bragging about having sent you off for an abortion,' Wallace continued with strong distaste. 'That didn't make sense to me. Drew was infatuated with you and he should've been eager to marry you. The most obvious explanation was that your child was *not* his...and I didn't have to look far to see that Leo was not behaving like a disinterested bystander.'

'How *did* he behave?' Angie was lured into asking.

Wallace cast knowing eyes over her unwittingly expressive face. 'Still Leo's most devoted admirer, aren't you?' he said with galling amusement. 'I'll say one thing for you, Angie—you're not flighty. You've got staying power, and I admire that in a woman.'

The door opened and her father came in with the day's post.

Wallace gave him a tired but surprisingly warm smile of

appreciation. 'Brown, you crafty old codger…letting loose Jake was a master-stroke of ingenuity!'

'Thank you, sir.'

Angie absorbed that exchange with shaken eyes. Her son's timely appearance in the hall had evidently not been the lucky chance she had assumed it to be.

'It certainly lessened the damage,' Wallace said approvingly.

'Quite so, sir…and after some time spent in the soothing company of his American lady Mr Drew will find it quite possible to pretend it never happened.'

'You think he'll be back for Christmas?' Wallace smothered a yawn with a frail hand, and he looked anxious.

'Oh, yes, sir. I shouldn't worry about that.' A surprisingly cynical twist briefly slanted her father's mouth as he picked up a mohair rug and almost tenderly spread it over Wallace's lap.

'I do so wish I could be proud of the boy,' the old man confided heavily. 'Leo's as straight as a die, nothing of the bad egg about him… One out of two; shouldn't complain, should I?'

In an undeniable daze, well aware that she had been quite forgotten about, Angie crept back to the door. Yet she knew that she would never forget that glimpse of Wallace and her father comfortably engaged in the candid dialogue of two older men who had known each other all their lives. For the first time, she had seen that the formal distance they maintained in public was a very poor indicator of the nature of their relationship, and that behind her father's loyalty lay a very real affection.

Afraid to go upstairs in case she ran into Leo and the tension between them exploded in Jake's presence, Angie headed through the green baize door for the first time since her arrival and slammed straight into her stepmother, a small, thin woman in her late fifties with greying hair and rather protuberant eyes.

'Angie...oh!' Emily gasped, looking hunted and dismayed.

'Thank you for sitting up with me last night—'

'Do you know where Mr Leo is?' Emily interrupted shrilly.

'He's with Jake upstairs...I think. If you've got a message for him, I should give it to Dad...' Her voice trailed away in surprise as the older woman simply scurried on past her with what could have been a stifled sob.

Angie hesitated, wondering if she ought to go after her stepmother, but she was in no mood after so traumatic a morning to deal with anyone. She would see Emily later. She hurried on past the kitchens, which were noisy with the busy feet and chatter of lunchtime activity. At the end of the long, flagstoned corridor, she dived into the butler's room to borrow her father's overcoat off the back of the door.

It was a new coat, she noted in some surprise, the cloth heavy and expensive. Maybe it had been a misfit for Wallace. She dug her arms into the sleeves while she scanned the contents of the key cupboard. A minute later she had located the key she sought, and she headed for the old servants' tunnel. It was as dark and dank as it had ever been, created over a century earlier to enable the servants and estate workers to enter the house without intruding into the gardens above, and thus offending the eyes of the family and their guests. Now the tunnel provided a very useful and concealed short-cut into the grounds.

She dug her hands into her pockets. Beyond the old ice house she slanted off on the path to the lake. One of Drew's least successful ideas had been the transformation of the Folly into self-catering tourist accommodation. Blithely ignoring his grandfather's love of privacy, Drew had spent a small fortune on the conversion.

'Honeymooners will love it!' he had forecast, putting in

a Jacuzzi with gold taps and a bed the size of a small football pitch.

But nobody had ever got the chance to stay there. Apart from Leo. She walked by the lake, no longer seeing the wind-blown grass and the bare trees but remembering instead the lushness of that early summer two and a half years earlier, the glory of the wild flowers, the drugging heat of midday…and Leo miraculously waiting for her…

'Join me,' he had suggested casually, indicating the elaborate picnic hamper resting on the rug. 'Today, I start life anew.'

Leo had been far from sober and dangerously volatile but, in her excitement, she hadn't seen that, had only registered that he was finally paying attention to her and expressing a desire for her company. With her father safely distant in London, Angie had spent the entirety of the preceding week throwing herself in Leo's path with increasing desperation, waking up every day in terror of hearing that he was returning to Greece.

But once ensconced on that cashmere rug, headily conscious of Leo's smouldering appraisal and vainly aware that most men considered her beautiful, Angie had been on a triumphant high, and ripe for a rude awakening to the harsher realities of life. And Leo had been right on one count—nothing that had happened that weekend had been on Angie's agenda.

'You remind me of a little cat lapping cream,' Leo had confided, reaching for her with indolently amused confidence and kissing her breathless.

She had had no control over the incredibly powerful physical feelings he'd aroused in her. Leo had not been remotely like the admiring, unsophisticated young men whom she had easily held at a distance. Sooner than she cared to recall, Leo had carried her into the Folly and made love to her with a wild, passionate impatience that had taken her by shock and storm.

Remembering how she had behaved still made Angie feel quite sick and shaky. She must have seemed so shameless, so pathetically obsessed. In her lowest moments, she sometimes wondered if Leo had gone to bed with her just to get rid of her.

Withdrawing the key, she stuck it into the door of the Folly and walked inside. Dismay stilled her in her tracks. All the evidence of Drew's conversion had gone. The building had been returned to its former purpose—a viewpoint on the hill above the lake, a comfortable place to sit even on a cold day. She mounted the stone staircase in the corner and surveyed the empty room above. Then, suddenly, she was flying downstairs and back out into the cold fresh air, scalding tears of regret running down her face and an agony of pain mushrooming up inside her.

She had been so happy that weekend, and so stupid that she had believed he was happy too!

'I like a woman who knows what she wants...as long as it's what I want too...and it was, it *was*,' Leo had confided with tender satisfaction as he'd gazed intently down at her, seemingly revelling in the tidal wave of affection and warmth she had been engulfing him in. 'And I like it even more when you look at me as if I'm the very centre of your universe...'

Dear God, how could he *ever* have asked her if she had used him as bait to make Drew jealous? She hadn't been able to hide her feelings that weekend, had been so helplessly, deliriously content—like a lost puppy finally finding its way home, she reflected, hating herself and just about the whole world at that instant, and scrubbing at her wet cheeks with feverishly unsteady hands.

How could she go on loving Leo when he had never, ever wanted her in the first place? And now he hated her like poison...of course he did! What male would welcome the fruit of a casual sexual encounter with a woman who meant nothing to him? But Leo, famed in the family for

his sense of honour, would love and accept his son because
Jake was an innocent victim of his mother's irresponsible
behaviour.

The crack of a snapping twig broke through Angie's
brooding, miserable thoughts and she whirled round. Leo
fell still under the cover of the trees, his hooded dark gaze
disturbingly level as he studied her. Angie snatched one
appalled look at him and whipped her reddened eyes away
again. He must have seen her from the house and, doubtless, had followed her up here to stage a showdown where
nobody would be likely to hear them. She braced herself
for the onslaught of bitter recriminations.

'Jake fell asleep in the middle of his lunch. I over-tired
him,' Leo said prosaically.

Angie blinked, hands stuffed deep into her pockets,
shoulders rigid with strain.

'It would be complete hypocrisy for me to bemoan his
existence,' Leo mused, almost as if he were talking out loud
to himself. 'He is a part of me, he is my son and, now that
the shock has faded a little, I have to confess that I am
delighted with him. I could be very angry that I missed out
on the first years of his life, but what would be the point?'

Totally bemused by what she was hearing, Angie found
herself gaping at him.

'It would've been much easier for you to have an abortion.' A grim smile of acknowledgement curved Leo's
wide, sensual mouth. 'But you didn't. I have to be grateful
for that.'

'Grateful...?' Angie parroted, so deeply shaken by the
concept that she could barely frame the word.

'I was equally grateful for your candour earlier.' Leo
continued to watch her with disturbing intensity, spiky
black lashes low on his penetrating dark eyes. 'Few women
would admit that they cold-bloodedly set out to try and
entrap a rich husband.'

Angie jolted back into life and flushed to the roots of her

hair. 'I…I…' she began, but she got no further because disabusing him of the conviction that she had been a committed, calculating little gold-digger would entail admitting that she had been madly in love with him—and, even worse, actually dumb enough to believe that she could miraculously replace the baby daughter he had lost, and thereafter bask in his warm and devoted appreciation.

In the electric silence, Leo regarded her expectantly, a black brow slightly raised as he waited for a further response.

'Yes, well,' Angie finally mumbled with a jerky shrug. 'Now you know.'

'So why didn't you ever make a bid to collect on your fertility?'

Angie tensed in dismay, not having been prepared for that very obvious question.

'You see, I'm having something of a problem understanding that aspect,' Leo confided softly. 'Wallace might in the heat of temper have forged that ridiculous deal with you, but all you had to do was contact me. Obviously there would've been no question of a prosecution. Your pregnancy gave you a fistful of aces, yet for some peculiar reason you made no attempt to play them.'

Angie squirmed. Leo had started out by allaying her worst fears, and had then cruelly pounced when she was a sitting duck. She didn't feel equal to the challenge of searching questions for clarification of what had motivated her at the time.

The silence lingered and grew until it clawed at her nerves.

'I just couldn't face telling you that I was pregnant…OK?' she shot back in the sudden desperation that swiftly translated into temper. 'In fact, after the way you treated me, I would've sooner drunk cyanide!'

'That seems reasonably comprehensive,' Leo responded with considerable irony, glittering dark eyes resting coolly on her hectically flushed and defiant face. 'I dented your ego and nothing, not even greed or ambition, could somehow persuade you to put my son's needs ahead of your own wounded pride.'

Angie winced and spun her head away. 'I wondered how long it would take you to start talking like that.'

'You're quite right,' Leo slotted in in unsettling agreement. 'Talk of that nature is most unproductive. And this *is*, after all, that very special moment when all that keen plotting and planning of two and a half years ago, all that assiduous tracking, hunting and tempting, leads to what now seems its almost inevitable conclusion...'

Every silky word hitting its shrinking target, Angie's strained blue eyes skimmed back to him in growing bewilderment.

Leo's brilliant dark gaze held hers fast. 'I can only legitimise my son's birth by marrying you.' A glimmer of a hard smile slanted his lips as he took in her utter stupefaction at his making that point. 'And I intend to carry through on that absolute necessity. Nobody will get the chance to call my son an "embarrassing little mistake" ever again!'

CHAPTER EIGHT

'YOU'RE asking me to m-marry you?' Angie stammered in frank astonishment.

'Not asking—*telling* you.' In emphasis of that not so subtle distinction, Leo closed the distance between them and stilled mere inches from her, his hard, dark features set with relentless determination. 'We are getting married.'

Angie swallowed with difficulty and simply gaped at him. Here, at least, was confirmation that there could be no other woman in Leo's life.

'*Before* the tabloids dream up crashingly crude and comic headlines about the butler's daughter, the Demetrios love-child and droit du seigneur in the steamy depths of Devon,' Leo clarified with a slashing twist of his sardonic mouth. 'Before Jake or anyone else starts asking awkward questions. And, last but not least, so that I can have full access to and rights over my own child!'

Slowly, Angie brought her lower lip up into contact with the upper again. It took considerable courage even to do that with Leo standing over her in the most intimidating fashion, bold dark eyes waiting to pounce on the smallest sign of opposition.

'But—'

'But *nothing*!' Leo blazed down at her with explosive menace. 'You owe it to your son and you owe it to me!'

Angie tried to retreat a step, but Leo was ready for that too. His hands shot out and entrapped hers, imprisoning her to the spot. Volatile dark eyes struck hers like a shower of lightning sparks. 'And let us not pretend that sharing a marital bed is likely to be a huge sacrifice for either of us. While you console yourself with my wealth, I will console myself with your beautiful body…I think it sounds like a match made in heaven, *pethi mou*.'

He backed her up against one of the pillars supporting the Folly's porticoed entrance, freed her hands and settled his own on the feminine swell of her hips. Angie shivered violently, legs weak as water, brain power in stunned suspension, the glorious heat and feel of Leo's lean, muscular body against her yielding softness provoking the most shattering surge of raw excitement inside her.

'Leo…' she whispered almost pleadingly.

Eyes burning pure gold, he pushed back the coat and skimmed long, lean fingers slowly up the straining length of her trembling thighs. She shuddered, leant back, throat extending. He took the invitation she offered with a wild, hot hunger that electrified her, crushing her mouth under his, and then, with a ragged groan, he jerked back from her. Angie's eyes opened again, defenceless in their confusion. It was like recovering consciousness after a stunning blow to the head.

Leo expelled his breath in a pent-up hiss. '*Theos*…we're in full view of the house!'

Angie flushed with mortified colour and looked away, fighting to regain control of her quivering body.

'I can't keep my hands off you,' Leo gritted half under his breath. 'But I shouldn't start things I can't finish and, to satisfy Wallace, we have a Christmas tree to choose.'

'A Ch-Christmas tree…?' Angie mumbled, wide-eyed.

'Tradition, Angie,' Leo imparted in stern reproof as he eased her off the pillar, smoothed down her skirt and rearranged her father's coat since it was perfectly obvious she was in no state to do it herself. He urged her back down the path. 'My grandfather is a stickler for tradition. As the future mistress of the Court, you get to pick the tree and watch me chop it down.'

'I haven't said I'll marry you.'

'I can't think of a single reason why you should refuse.'

You don't love me. Her warm colour bled away on that stark truth. Leo, her hero from adolescence, her one and only lover and the father of her child. He had been her most destructive weakness from the age of thirteen. But to be Leo's wife, to possess him in body and legality, if not in soul…to turn over in bed at night and find him…to have the right to lift the phone and hear his voice whenever she felt like it… A rush of intoxicating emotion gripped Angie.

'All right…I'll marry you.' Shamefaced, she addressed the ground at her feet, horribly conscious of that overpowering surge of love and its lack of pride or conscience.

'Of course you will…I rather took agreement for granted when you leant back against that pillar and offered yourself to me in broad daylight.'

Crimson-cheeked, Angie flung up her head and met spectacular dark eyes ablaze with sharply disconcerting amusement. That shook her. But then nothing Leo had said or done over the past minutes had even come close to matching her expectations, she conceded dazedly as he walked her across the bridge over the lake.

It was as if there was a core of joyous vibrancy now lit deep inside him and it was a major effort for him to keep it concealed. It was Jake, of course. Her son had walked right into Leo's heart and immediately found a place there as she herself had never managed to do. Her shoulders drooped, the high-wire tension that had kept her on edge for hours draining away.

'I'll make arrangements for a special licence,' Leo announced as they crunched across the gravel at the front of the Court. 'We'll get the ceremony out of the way before Christmas—'

'*Before* Christmas?' Angie gasped.

'Christmas Eve, if the rector's agreeable. A quiet family ceremony. You'll need a ring, not to mention a new wardrobe,' Leo mused reflectively. 'Then there's the matter of Jake's Christmas presents. I know it's far from cool, but I can hardly wait to sack the toy shops. We'll fly up to London tomorrow.'

'Yes,' Angie muttered rather weakly, conscious of her growing exhaustion as they entered the house.

Her father was waiting in the Great Hall, Emily beside him, her face pinched and pale, her eyes evasive. 'Could we have a word with you, sir?' he asked stiffly.

Belatedly recalling that her stepmother had been looking for Leo earlier, Angie tensed. A frown line of surprise and unease divided her brows but, with a faint smile, Leo settled a hand on her taut spine and swept her with him into the study.

The door hadn't even closed before Emily broke into speech.

'It wasn't Angie who stole those things... I let her take the b-blame,' her stepmother stammered in a tearful rush, 'but I was the one who took them and sold them. Angie was trying to put the miniature back when Mr Wallace found her with it!'

Angie's stunned gaze leapt from her father's impenetrable gravity to her stepmother's open terror and then to Leo's stasis in the centre of the room.

'Mr Neville has known the truth for a long time,' Samuel Brown admitted tautly.

Angie stiffened in shock, finally understanding why Wallace had found it possible to welcome her so warmly back into his home.

His magnificent bone structure rigid, Leo studied his butler incredulously. 'My grandfather *knew*?'

'My wife didn't confide in me until she was in hospital, and by—'

'When was Emily in hospital?' Angie broke in anxiously.

'A few months after you left, I had a nervous breakdown,' her stepmother confided tightly.

'Why wasn't I told about all this?' Leo demanded rawly.

'By the time I was able to tell Mr Wallace what Emily

had done, the Court had already been sold to you, sir,' Samuel explained. 'Mr Wallace advised us to keep quiet.'

'To keep quiet,' Leo echoed half under his breath, a perceptible shudder racking him. 'My grandfather advised you not to tell me?'

'Mr Wallace believed that you would sack me, and it would've been no more than we deserved... But at the time, with my wife ill and no savings to fall back on...' the older man framed with growing difficulty.

'Simon Legree or Judge Jeffreys...take your pick,' Leo filled in grimly. 'What a salutary experience it is to see myself through the eyes of others!'

Angie crossed the room to wrap her arms round her petrified stepmother and give her a soothing hug. 'It's all right, Em,' she said gently while shooting Leo a positively pleading look. 'Leo understands. He isn't angry. It's all over and done with now.'

Her father was poker-straight, but sickly pale. 'Obviously I'm tendering my resignation, sir.'

'I'm marrying your daughter, Samuel. I'm afraid you're stuck with this family for the rest of your days.'

'Marrying my daughter?' The older man was visibly shaken by the announcement.

'Yes...we're getting married,' Angie confirmed.

A slow smile blossomed on her father's strained face. 'That's wonderful news.' He hesitated then, discomfiture with this new situation clearly overtaking him almost as quickly. 'I'll take Emily downstairs now, if I may? Facing up to this has taken a lot out of her, sir.'

Silence fell as they left the room. Angie's gaze connected apprehensively with Leo's now blatant stare of outraged condemnation. 'I would've told you once we were married!' she asserted.

'Thank you for that slender vote of confidence!' Leo grated with a curled lip. 'Why the hell didn't you just tell me last week?'

'Well, for a start, I didn't know that Emily had even owned up to my father,' Angie groaned, her head beginning to ache. 'And it wasn't my story to tell. It wasn't me who was going to suffer if you reacted badly and decided to prosecute and threw the two of them out of the house.'

'So instead you let me call you a thief.' His mouth hard as iron, Leo thrust raking, not quite steady fingers through his glossy black hair.

Angie hastened to explain why her stepmother had gone so wildly off the rails. Emily had got into secret debt with a credit card. Too ashamed to confide in her husband, and conscious that their tiny budget would never stretch to meet the payments being demanded, desperation had driven her to stealing. She had sold everything for next to nothing to an unscrupulous trader in a local market. By pure chance, Angie had found the miniature portrait hidden in the flat. After dragging the whole sorry story out of the terrified older woman, Angie had made the last payment on the card, using her savings from a part-time job she had had.

'Your father's salary was static for almost fifteen years,' Leo volunteered flatly. 'He didn't complain, and it wasn't noticed until my staff took over and examined the household accounts. I imagine that goes some way to explaining why your stepmother got herself into a mess.'

He understood. He genuinely understood. Angie felt quite sick with relief and, simultaneously, her legs began shaking beneath her. Those thefts had hung round her neck like an albatross for *so* long. She had never dared to hope that Emily would work up the courage to confess the truth to anyone, had even feared that Leo might not believe her if she did choose to speak up.

'I never doubted your guilt,' Leo bit out roughly, his lean, strong features fiercely taut as he made that grudging but honest admission. 'When I saw the disgusting state of your father's flat two years ago, I was appalled. Wallace hadn't been down there in twenty years, and wouldn't even have thought to check up. I understood your resentment on your family's behalf, and for that reason I accepted that you were the thief.'

Angie now had a thumping tension headache, and her weary shoulders sagged. 'I'm sorry I couldn't risk telling you the truth—'

'And now I know everything, do I?' Leo prompted with a sudden soft and disturbing quietness, brilliant eyes resting on her pale, drawn profile. 'The butler's daughter chose not to steal but instead set her sights squarely and very sensibly on marrying the richest prospect in the family?'

'I'm not feeling very well, Leo,' she mumbled, pushing her hair off her damp brow as a wave of dismaying dizziness ran over her.

'Because you haven't the wit of a flea when it comes to looking after yourself.' Striding forward, Leo swept her swaying figure up into his powerful arms. 'You were ill last night...so what do you do? You skip lunch, stand around in temperatures below freezing for hours and, for good measure, neglect to button up that wretched coat. There is this huge horrific gap inside you where other people have common sense...and the extraordinary thing is that at this moment *I'm* feeling tremendous!'

'Because of Jake,' she mumbled miserably.

'Don't whine, *pethi mou*...you've caught yourself a billionaire.'

'I wasn't whining.'

'It sounded remarkably like a whine to me. Relax; we'll reschedule the historic choosing of the tree until tomorrow. Even Wallace will understand that I don't want a bride on the brink of collapse. Right now, you will eat and then sleep.'

Angie was too utterly exhausted to argue. It had been the most emotionally draining day of her life, and now that the artificial stimulant of stress had been removed she could barely keep her heavy eyes open.

*   *   *

Angie breakfasted in bed the next morning, feeling deliciously pampered and incredibly insouciant. She had slept the clock round. She was seeing the whole world through rose-coloured glasses. She was going to marry the man she loved... Leo was right—whining would be most inappropriate.

As soon as she was dressed, she took Jake down to the basement where her father and stepmother lived in their self-contained flat.

'You're in for a surprise,' her father warned as he opened the smart new front door.

She certainly was. The damp and cramped accommodation she recalled had been extended and transformed into a light, bright and comfortably furnished home.

'Mr Leo had it all done up just for us,' Samuel Brown explained. 'He increased my salary too...he's been a very generous employer.'

The previous day's distress overcome, Emily smiled uncertainly at Angie. 'I feel so much better now it's all come out,' she admitted.

'It *had* to be sorted out once you came back,' her father pointed out awkwardly to Angie. 'I would never have allowed you to take the blame for those thefts, but by the time I found out that you had you were gone and Mr Leo owned the Court. I didn't feel right about keeping quiet—'

'It's all right, Dad. With Em ill, you had enough to worry about,' Angie reassured him hurriedly.

'Like the police, everyone else thinks that the thief was never caught, but most of the stolen items *were* recovered,' her father stressed.

'How do you feel about me marrying Leo?' Angie asked baldly.

'I'm happy for you, of course I am...but it'll take some getting used to,' Samuel Brown admitted with a rueful smile.

Angie went back upstairs to get Jake's coat, brimming

happiness adding a bounce to her step. When she came down again on the same wave of euphoria, Leo was waiting in the Great Hall for her. Tall, dark, spectacular, she thought giddily. He extended an unfamiliar coat to her in much the same way as a matador might have flourished his cape at a bull.

'Where did you borrow this?' Having put on the coat, Angie twisted round to look at herself in the nearest mirror, loving the fact that the coat was very long and black and dramatic, and, lifting the luxurious furry collar up round her face, feeling like Anna Karenina.

'It was an impulse buy.'

Angie stroked the soft cashmere with covetous hands and twirled again, eyes starry. 'It's just breathtaking,' she told him chokily, because she couldn't remember when she had last had anything to wear that she really liked, never mind loved.

'Changed your attitude to Greeks bearing gifts?'

'Depends what you want in return,' she teased daringly as they walked out to the Range Rover outside.

'You...tonight,' Leo said succinctly.

Angie's face flamed and she sent him a speaking glance of shaken reproach.

'My wealth in exchange for your body,' Leo reminded her without a flicker of remorse, stunningly dark eyes gleaming over her. 'It's really not a sensitive or deeply meaningful exchange, Angie...but I'm certainly not complaining. What male in his right mind would? After all, if you were in love with me, great feats of romantic effort would be expected from me.'

'I think you'd find yourself facing an impossible challenge,' Angie responded thinly, mouth flat, eyes stony but suspiciously bright.

CHAPTER NINE

'YOU'VE got completely the wrong idea about why I'm marrying you,' Angie told Leo tremulously, pacing up and down on the flattened grass. 'Oh, do stop hacking at that wretched tree for a minute!'

Leo straightened, whipcord muscles rippling beneath the thin, damp silk of his shirt. Angie became so busy running absorbed and helplessly appreciative eyes over his magnificent physique, she very nearly tripped over a log. He looked hot and sweaty and unbelievably sexy. She felt like a Stone Age woman surveying the king of the gene pool, and shivered deliciously while she imagined Leo carrying her back to some wintry, prehistoric cave and ravishing her to within an inch of her life. Colour fluctuating wildly, eyes glowing like sapphires, Angie emerged from that vision, shocked rigid by it, and was appalled to find Leo studying her with an enquiringly raised brow.

'I'm listening,' he encouraged silkily. 'You said I had the wrong idea about—'

'Oh, yes,' Angie recalled jerkily, and commenced pacing in a tortured circle again while Jake jumped on and off the log. 'As I was saying...I'm marrying you for some very good reasons—'

'Name them.' Leo struck the twenty-foot-tall tree another resounding blow with the axe.

'One, Jake needs a father...two, I want him to have absolutely the very best of everything...three...' Angie trailed off, sidetracked by a complete inability to drag her eyes from the powerful muscles flexing in Leo's long, denim-clad thighs, and becoming increasingly breathless and disjointed in her delivery.

'Three?' Leo prompted, not even breathing hard.

'You're so fit...I mean...' Throwing him a flustered look, Angie started frantically pacing again. 'I mean, you're healthy—that's a plus too! Obviously I wouldn't want to marry someone who was likely to peg out on me.'

'Don't worry...I won't peg out on you tonight, and I do see that that would be a matter of concern to you when tonight is just about all you can think about.' Leo gave the shuddering, leaning trunk a sudden forceful thrust, and the Scots pine went crashing down in thunderous emphasis.

Jake leapt up and down in awed appreciation of the sight, and then went careening round the fallen tree with excited whoops. Angie dug trembling hands into her pockets and affected not to have heard that last awesomely shrewd assurance. She could feel her face burning with chagrined colour, and Leo, watching her, was no doubt highly amused by her lack of sophistication and her inability to hide her response to him.

'I just didn't want you thinking that...' she began awkwardly again.

'It's not a problem, Angie. Petrina married me for my money too, but she was considerably less honest about it.'

Sheer astonishment paralysed Angie to the spot.

Having delivered that revelation in the most offhand manner, Leo vented a sudden, startled expletive and roared, 'Jake...no!' as he moved with the speed of light to prevent the toddler from getting his eager hands on the axe lying on the ground.

Shocked by that roar, Jake went off into frightened howls. Leo lifted him up and hugged him in consolation.

'You should've been watching him,' he said quite unnecessarily because Angie was already feeling all the guilt of a mother whose attention had strayed.

'You shouldn't have left the axe where he could get hold of it!' Angie was not to be outdone.

The tree would be delivered to the house and set up in

the Great Hall to be dressed. A mutually dissatisfied silence reigned as they climbed back into the Range Rover, but Angie could think of nothing but that staggering statement that Petrina had married him for his wealth.

'I thought Petrina was an heiress,' she said abruptly as they drew up in front of the house.

'I neglected to run a credit check on my in-laws. Her father's companies were in serious trouble. The day after the wedding—which Petrina had pushed forward on his behalf—I was informed that it was my duty to solve his problems. The experience left me with few illusions.' Leo sprang out of the car.

'When are we leaving?'

'I need a shower.' Reflective dark eyes rested on her, amusement slanting his mouth. 'You can take your coat off for a while. I doubt if it will run away.'

After an early lunch, enlivened by Wallace's good humour, they flew up to London in the helicopter with Leo at the controls. Jake was ecstatic, but Angie spent most of the trip calming Harriet Davis, who was a nervous flyer. At the airport, they split up. Jake and his nanny were going to the town house while Leo took Angie to Cartier.

Half an hour later, they were outside on the pavement again. A pair of matching wedding rings had been bought. But Angie was also the stunned owner of an opulent sapphire and diamond engagement ring, not to mention the exquisite gold watch and the two pairs of earrings which had somehow happened to attract Leo's attention. Angie, who had never seen anyone buy so much at such speed, was in shock.

'I really wasn't expecting an engagement ring,' she confided breathlessly as she scrambled back into the limousine, turning her hand this way and that to catch the light in the precious gems, quite unable to hide the sheen of dreamy pleasure in her eyes.

'Naturally I will make every effort to ensure that this relationship appears normal to other people,' Leo drawled almost gently.

The sparkle went right out of Angie's engagement ring even as she looked at it. Her buoyancy vanished as if he had plunged a hat pin into the balloon of happiness swelling inside her heart.

'I've also instructed my lawyers to draw up a pre-nuptial agreement,' Leo continued, his lustrous dark gaze intent on her startled face. 'It will tie you up so tight that if I should ever think of divorcing you you will be down on your knees begging me to change my mind!'

'Excuse me?' A deep flush had burned Angie's cheek-bones to carmine.

Leo elevated an ebony brow. 'It would be very foolish of me not to restrict your boundaries. In a marriage where the bonds are strictly of a convenient nature, I have to con-sider the possibility that your attention might stray—'

'We haven't even got married yet!' Angie blistered back at him in disbelief. 'And you're talking about my attention straying?'

'I like to consider every conceivable angle. I'm a businessman,' Leo pointed out with a fluid shrug.

Angie was cut to the bone, but she was also furious with him. He was still convinced she was after his wretched money! But then perhaps she needed that reminder to bring her back down to solid earth again, she reflected with shrinking self-loathing. From the moment Leo had asked her to marry him, the larger part of her brain had been wheeling and dipping in some heavenly never-never land. Why? Marrying Leo had always been her dream. Only now she had to face the fact that, while she had always loved him, he had never loved her, and that his preparations for the wedding had nothing to do with either romance or cele-bration.

He insisted on taking her shopping for clothes. Angie's

temper steadily rose. She was starting to feel like a possession to be paraded, an inanimate object to be suitably dressed and presented for public consumption. In an exclusive salon, while Leo sat in a gilded chair, nursing a glass of mulled wine, Angie tried on one fabulously expensive outfit after another.

She stalked in and out of the changing room, quite magnificent in her growing rage, and sashayed, twirled and flounced in three-inch heels, striving to make him feel uncomfortable. But, impervious to her feelings, Leo lounged back, indolently relaxed, and watched her with deeply appreciative night-dark eyes, lush black lashes sinking lower and lower to give him a deceptively sleepy look.

'Keep that on,' he murmured when she emerged in a scarlet suit with black facings that made a superb frame for the long, lithe shape of her figure. 'What about lingerie?'

Angie cast him a murderous look since it was perfectly obvious to her that Leo was living out the worst kind of male fantasy. 'I'll see to that when I'm on my own.'

'I'm enjoying myself,' Leo confided without shame.

'I want a wedding dress,' Angie told him from between clenched teeth. 'I want a wedding dress with yards and yards of train, and a veil and flowers and loads of lace—'

'Good idea,' Leo slotted in approvingly. 'Wallace will revel in all the traditional bridal trimmings, but we don't have time today.'

'I should wear black with little pound signs printed all over it!' Angie hissed furiously under her breath. 'That's what you deserve.'

Leo cast her a vibrantly amused look. 'Oh, I think I know exactly what I deserve, and I can hardly contain my ardour, *pethi mou*.'

Face flaming with hot colour and every pulse in her taut body humming, Angie was the one to break that sizzlingly sensual visual connection first. She returned to the spacious cubicle to run back carefully through the various outfits she had decided to take, and agonise over one or two borderline choices. It took her some time, and, after that, it gave her the most truly enormous thrill to stroll through to the shoe and handbag department and just point at what she liked.

'You can have anything you want,' Leo had stressed. '*Anything*…and don't you dare look at the prices!'

All the Christmas lights were on when they emerged back onto the street. Multicoloured, bright and beautiful, lighting up the darkening sky and the bustling shoppers crowding the pavements, they stopped Angie in her tracks. 'Gorgeous, aren't they?' she said wistfully.

'Yes.' Leo wasn't looking at the lights, he was looking at her, but she was sublimely unaware of the fact.

'I've always been a bit childish about Christmas,' she muttered, suddenly embarrassed.

'That's not without its charm.' With a slow smile, Leo urged her back into the waiting limousine. 'We have a date to keep with Jake in his bath.'

Forty minutes later, Angie stood back, watching Leo happily dive-bombing plastic boats with a toy aeroplane while Jake squealed with delight and splashed water everywhere in his excitement. She could have dropped dead without Leo noticing, she thought miserably, ashamed and annoyed with herself for experiencing such strong pangs of envy.

He was going to be a wonderful father. Few men had the ability to get down and play at a toddler's level with honest enjoyment. But it was the tenderness, the caring that she could already see in that dark gaze trained on their son that wrenched most at her aching heart. Leo would never look at her like that. She would always be on the outside of the charmed circle of Leo's love—an adjunct, never a necessity.

They were going to be dining out, and she wanted to change. As soon as Jake was settled for the night, Angie went through to the adjoining bedroom and then stilled at the sight of Harriet's overnight bag on the bed. In silence, Leo strolled up behind her, closed his hand over hers and walked her back out again, down the corridor and into the master bedroom.

'In three days' time, we'll be married,' Leo delivered gently. 'I have no plans to tiptoe over creaking floorboards in my own home.'

Angie blushed fierily and hurried into the dressing room, opening doors until she found what she sought. A midnight blue shift dress of wonderful simplicity and elegance. As she emerged from the wardrobe, Leo pulled open three drawers in succession to reveal the soft jewel colours of silk and lace lingerie sets.

'I made my own selections while you were otherwise engaged,' he explained.

Head bent, Angie skated an uncertain finger over the nearest item, heat surging inside her at the knowledge that he had personally chosen such intimate apparel.

'You can be incredibly shy.' Leo laughed huskily, trailing a mocking forefinger across the tremulous fullness of her lower lip to awaken a tingling, intense awareness of his dominant masculinity. 'But it is still a challenge to believe that, in all the time you were with Drew, you didn't once say yes.'

Taken aback by that disturbingly soft and unsettling statement, Angie glanced up unwarily and clashed directly with searching dark golden eyes. Her breath feathered in her throat. 'Drew never *asked*.'

Derision glittered in Leo's steady perusal. 'Don't treat me like an idiot.'

Angie tilted her chin. 'We were friends. That's all I offered, and Drew accepted that.'

Leo looked supremely unimpressed by the explanation.

Angie spun angrily away. He couldn't believe that she had never slept with Drew. But, when she thought about it, she understood his reasoning. Leo didn't have the one missing piece that would have made sense of the puzzle: her love for him and his cousin's full awareness of it had kept Drew at arm's length.

'I've already given you my answer, and now I want to get dressed,' Angie said tautly.

Leo held her anxious gaze for several taut seconds and then, with a smile she didn't like at all, he inclined his arrogant dark head.

As he swung on his heel, Angie cleared her throat. 'And I don't ever want to be put through a second round of this conversation, Leo!'

'An honest response will forever close the subject.'

'You're jealous of Drew...I can't believe it!' Angie exclaimed helplessly. 'A man I don't even like any more...'

Leo flashed her a look of outraged censure over one broad shoulder. 'I...jealous of Drew?' he slung back at her grittily. 'Are you out of your mind?'

'I'm really glad that you're not the jealous type,' Angie managed, and averted her eyes lest they betray her extreme lack of honesty.

In three days' time, she would become the wife of a ferociously jealous and possessive male. The darker passions seethed below that cool, sophisticated surface of his. Angie had the most extraordinary desire to wrap her arms round him and tell him that she adored him, but as she recalled that pre-nuptial agreement he had mentioned and the engagement ring that she had only received for the edification of the general public the desire to give generously of her love withered utterly on the vine.

She got dressed in the *en suite* bathroom and emerged to find that Leo had already gone downstairs. As she descended the staircase, she saw him waiting in the hall. Tall, dark, devastating. Her susceptible heart leapt. There he was, finally wearing a dinner jacket for *her*, and, for an appalled moment, she was honestly afraid that the upsurge of emotion inside her might make her cry.

'You look breathtaking,' Leo murmured huskily.

'Yeah, well…you bought the dress.' Angie grimaced to hold the tears back, and surreptitiously sniffed. And demanded the right to take me out of it again, she couldn't help thinking, cheeks warming as she struggled not to mentally anticipate the evening's closing agenda.

Leo burst out laughing.

'What's so funny?'

He wrapped her into her cashmere coat. 'It wouldn't translate very well.'

He took her to an extremely smart restaurant. Heads turned and eyes lingered on their entrance. They made a striking couple. A dozen people murmured greetings to Leo, their curiosity about his beautiful blonde companion unconcealed. Leo smiled and nodded in recognition, but he didn't once pause.

'I gather this is part and parcel of the making - the - relationship - look - normal - and - introducing - me - to - the - public - eye bit,' Angie condemned tightly. 'Some first date, Leo!'

'Our first date took place a long time ago. It was a picnic by the lake,' Leo responded silkily. 'We may not actually have eaten anything out of that hamper until late in the evening, but it's the one and only date that I've ever had that lasted an entire weekend.'

Face heating at that mortifying reminder, Angie hid behind her menu until a tiny, delicate woven basket of wild flowers was delivered to their table. She blinked in bemusement at the attached card bearing Leo's signature. Where the heck had he got wild flowers in the middle of winter? She found she *had* to ask.

'I had them flown in from a warmer climate.'

'Oh…' There had been wild flowers that day by the lake, the scent of the crushed blooms sweet and heady in the hot, still air as she'd lain in his arms… Surely nothing so specific as tender memory could have prompted his gesture?

During the first course, Leo rested bold dark eyes resolutely on her. 'I planned the whole exercise. I ordered the hamper and then I lay in wait for you, secure in the knowledge that *you* would find *me*.'

Angie very nearly choked on a luscious cube of melon.

Leo poured her a glass of iced water. 'I have to confess that I didn't have a single decent intention in my head.'

Coughing and spluttering into her napkin, Angie pushed back her plate and snatched at the glass to sip the water and soothe her convulsing throat muscles.

'And I had to punish you for infiltrating my every sexual fantasy. I was also feeling very guilty. I was seven months out of a marriage which had been a disaster in the bedroom,' Leo continued with devastating candour. 'And there you were, brazenly ignoring all my keep-off signals, and targeting me with a single-minded tenacity of purpose that was so blatant—'

'Please don't say any more, Leo,' Angie whispered, verbally on her knees and pleading as she drank down great gulps of iced water, cheeks hot enough to fry eggs on.

'So unashamed and so *honest*, it was a very powerful draw for me.'

Her brow furrowed as she ran back over that last sentence.

Leo vented a grim laugh of amusement. '*Ohi*...no, you didn't realise that, did you? That all the time I was freezing you out on another level I was reluctantly impressed and attracted by your persistence?'

'It didn't show.' Angie's gaze was riveted to the dark splendour of his, her heartbeat speeding up.

'I didn't even acknowledge it to myself then,' Leo conceded, his dark, deep drawl husky. 'But Petrina never wanted me like that. She wasn't capable of that kind of passion. You were, and you seemed to be offering me exactly what I wanted and needed.'

Heated colour blossomed afresh in her cheeks yet she

was held fast by the brooding, magnetic intensity of his stare.

An odd little silence fell, thick and heavy. Angie licked nervously at her dry lower lip. Watching her, Leo flinched.

'Let's get out of here,' he breathed abruptly, a ragged, fevered edge to his voice. 'It was a cardinal error to start talking about *that* weekend in public!'

In astonishment, she tensed, but Leo was already rising, dark eyes blazing with a sexual hunger he made no attempt to conceal.

The *maître d'* surged towards their table. Angie stood up jerkily, her shaken gaze welded to Leo. He snaked a possessive arm around her trembling body and dismissed the older man's concern with an easy, wry reference to an overlooked appointment.

Dimly aware of the rush of curious comment as Leo swept her back outside, Angie's face burned, but she could no more have resisted Leo in that particular mood than she could have resisted the need to draw life-giving air into her lungs.

He signalled to his chauffeur across the street. 'My flowers, Leo...my flowers!' Angie cried in dismay. 'I forgot—'

She fell silent as a grinning waiter emerged from the restaurant with the precious little basket. Leo vented an incredulous laugh. 'But they're useless...they'll be dead in another couple of hours!'

Angie clutched the basket to her as if she was afraid it might be thrust in the nearest waste-paper bin. With a look of rueful amusement and a stifled, husky sound of impatience, Leo pulled her to him without warning and brought his mouth down in hot demand on hers. She went down into that wildly passionate kiss with buckling knees, and stumbled into the car after it in a welter of shell-shocked excitement.

'Don't come near me,' Leo advised hoarsely as the limo moved off again, street lights glancing over his spectacular bone structure, accentuating the harsh, taut slant of his cheekbones and the golden burn of his smouldering gaze. 'Not unless you want to be dragged down and ravished right here and now…plundered and pillaged by a male close to the edge.'

Angie shivered convulsively, her body boneless and utterly pliant as she shifted infinitesimally, the pounding pulse beat of desire sending helpless little tremors through her.

Leo gritted something raw in Greek. 'Don't look at me like that…it doesn't help!'

Dry-mouthed, Angie stared back at him, absorbing the splintering, ferocious tension he emanated.

'I'd do it… I'm not an English gentleman like my cousin. And I have this feeling that you are going to learn to make love in some very unusual places because sometimes, when I look at you, I think I *can't* wait…not another day, not another hour, not another *second*!' he groaned, and flung his arrogant dark head back, closing his eyes, dense black lashes almost hitting his cheekbones. 'And knowing that you feel the same way adds a whole new dimension to my agony!'

'You think I'm wanton, don't you?' Angie prompted chokily.

'Wanton works wonderfully well for me, Angie,' Leo confided raggedly. 'In fact, when you fix those huge blue eyes on me, my testosterone count probably hits danger levels. Going from a famine to a feast two and a half years ago was the most unnerving part of the whole experience!'

Unseen by him, Angie was cringing. She was learning a lot, but nothing that made comfortable listening. So the intimate side of his first marriage had been less than satisfactory. If she had ever been able to bring herself to consider that issue, she would have suspected that reality for herself. Leo was a very physical male, tactile, hot-blooded, spontaneous. Petrina had been cool and essentially narcissistic. But it hurt Angie a great deal to accept that all that had ever drawn Leo to her was his sexual frustration, his recognition of her as a willing bed partner likely to satisfy his needs with the minimum of fuss and demands.

'You were just a silly kid,' Leo breathed with startling abruptness as he lifted his head to look directly at her again, brilliant dark eyes innately shrewd and his accented drawl disturbingly rough. 'On the outside a woman, but inside one very reckless little girl. But I didn't see that...I didn't even realise you were still a teenager until it was too late.'

Angie had tensed. 'Didn't you?'

'I remembered you romping about in the background over the years...but, if you hadn't been so good on a horse, I'd never have noticed you at all,' he admitted bluntly. 'You were very, very careful not to tell me that you'd just finished school that summer. You talked about the job you were starting in August, but you never admitted that it would be your *first*.'

Angie studied her tightly linked hands, too guilty to meet his gaze. 'I was a full year older than everyone else in sixth year...I more or less lost the year that my mother died because I got behind with my work and I had to repeat a year. I wasn't *really* trying to hide my age from you.'

'Excuse me...you *were*,' Leo countered.

'I just w-wanted to seem more mature,' Angie protested.

'Oh, you managed that all right.' His expressive mouth quirked as the chauffeur opened the door beside her, letting in a flood of cool night air.

Angie scrambled out with intense relief. Leo unlocked the front door, thrust it wide. 'In fact you managed that right up until the magic moment when I realised that I was in bed with a virgin.'

Angie shed her coat and headed for the stairs at speed, escape from the extremely embarrassing nature of the conversation her only ambition.

'I never would have dreamt that a virgin could be such

a polished little temptress,' Leo whispered in her shrinking ear from behind, curving restraining hands round her slim hips when she attempted to take flight. 'Naturally I'd assumed that you were experienced.'

Temper stirring, Angie broke free of his hold and raced up to the landing. 'You certainly didn't complain when you found out I wasn't!'

Leo drew level with her, an aggressive strength and poise in his stance, long legs set slightly apart as he gazed down at her. 'A certain primitive streak in me rejoiced in the knowledge that I was your first lover...but when sanity returned I felt like a complete bastard.'

'Only you were careful not to feel bad until *after* you'd had what you wanted!' Bitter and accusing chagrin laced her every word.

'*Theos*...you get one idea in your head and then you stick to it like superglue! There are times when I could quite happily strangle you,' Leo confessed with raw impatience as he reached for her with hands that brooked no refusal and swept her up into his arms. 'But that is nothing to what I wanted to do to you when I saw you with Drew! And you smirked at me as if you were a cheap, malicious little—'

Biting off the rest of that wrathful sentence, he swore in Greek at a memory that still evidently whipped him on the raw. His arms tightening round her, he treated her to a grim look of condemnation for that past offence as he strode into his bedroom.

'I did not smirk...I *didn't*!' Angie gasped furiously. 'Put me down!'

'With pleasure...' Leo dropped her down on the well-sprung divan in an inelegant heap of splayed limbs, her hair flying everywhere. 'It's past time that we had a little plain speaking between us. Not something you excel at, *pethi mou*...but something you will learn to be really, really good at around me!'

'You think so?' Angie sliced back, clawing her wildly disordered hair off her outraged face.

'I *know* so. You accused me of ditching you like yesterday's newspaper. You talk and behave as if I took deliberate advantage of your innocence,' Leo launched down at her in an intimidating growl of censure. 'But we both know that you played a starring role in your own downfall. When a woman throws herself at a man, he sees a sexual invitation, not the opening chapter of a serious affair!'

'How *dare* you?' Angie was so mad at him, she was shaking.

'And perhaps you'd care to tell me how I could have continued that affair when everything that had already happened between us was utterly indefensible!' Leo bit out savagely. 'You were far too young. I was twenty-seven, you were nineteen.'

Angie flung her head back, eyes bright blue chips of fiery scorn. 'And I was the butler's daughter...let's not forget that!'

Leo shot her a menacing look that would have ground a lesser woman into the dust. 'Two generations back my family in Greece were fishermen, but I was raised to be proud of my roots. Open your eyes...these days social mobility is everywhere, and highly regarded!'

'But some of us prefer not to sleep our way to that regard!' Angie told him with a proud toss of her head as she swung her legs towards the edge of the bed.

'You stay where you are,' Leo told her with a warning flare in his intimidating gaze as he peeled off his dinner jacket in an impatient movement. 'We will have this out if it takes all night! We both betrayed our respective families' trust that weekend, but at least I acknowledge that I was in the wrong—*when* will you?'

Shaken by that pointed demand, Angie gulped, 'I did...I do, but—'

Leo sent his jacket sailing across the room onto a chair

as if she had given ground on a long-awaited concession. 'And when you appreciate that you have made a wrong step, do you then say to yourself, "This feels good, so even though it's wrong I'll keep on doing it"?'

Angie got even more flustered. 'No...but—'

'There is no *but*,' Leo slotted in fiercely. 'I did what I believed was right at that moment in time. Since I was not prepared to make a proper commitment to you, I ended it!'

'You crushed me...' Angie mumbled tightly.

Leo released his breath in a dark, driven hiss. 'It wouldn't have been fair to leave you with the impression that I might come back to you.'

A humourless laugh was squeezed from her thickened throat. 'You should be proud of yourself; you were very successful!'

'I *know*...' Leo gave that low-pitched agreement a strange, weighted significance, his lean, strong face shadowed and taut. 'I'm very thorough in most things that I set out to do. It was a crazy, wonderful weekend, but it became too intense too soon. I had to draw back to take stock for both our sakes.'

Suddenly, Angie couldn't bring herself to look at him. Tears sprang to her eyes. This was the real truth she was hearing now, she thought in agony. 'Too intense.' She had shown her feelings too openly, and no doubt he had registered what an embarrassment she could become. So 'wonderful' a weekend, but not one he had had any desire to repeat...not so wonderful after all.

The mattress gave slightly with his weight. With surprising gentleness, Leo looped the veil of her pale hair off her strained profile and let his knuckles brush softly across one taut cheekbone. 'You're such a baby sometimes...you just won't look before you leap. I'm not an impulsive man, but that weekend I seized the moment and I didn't see the consequences until it was too late. There was a price to be paid. I didn't *want* to hurt you—'

'But you did…you couldn't get away from me quickly enough!'

Leo closed a powerful arm round her rigid shoulders and forced her close. 'I didn't trust myself anywhere near you…'

Struggling for breath, terrified she might lose control and howl all over him, Angie thrust her damp face into his broad shoulder, dimly wondering how on earth she had ended up welded to his long, hard frame like a second skin, but receiving too much vicarious security from the embrace to have the will-power to move away.

'And I still don't,' Leo muttered in unexpected continuance, burying his mouth with a muffled groan in the scented hollow of her collarbone, and ensuring that every pulse in her body leapt into sudden, startled and treacherous life.

Leo lifted his head again. Angie pressed helpless fingers to the tiny pulse flickering like mad at the base of her throat. She was trembling without even being aware of it.

In the rushing silence, Leo reached behind her to pull down the zip on her dress. He eased it down over her arms, exposing the firm swell of her breasts, cupped in a blue lace bra and shifting with every jerky breath she snatched in. Slowly he pushed her back against the pillows.

Shimmering dark golden eyes roamed over her with intense male appreciation. He peeled the dress expertly down over her hips, drew it off and cast it aside. Then he slid fluidly off the bed and began to undress, ripping open the press studs on his shirt, revealing sun-bronzed skin and the rough pelt of black curls hazing his powerful pectoral muscles. He shrugged out of the garment, sleek brown shoulders emerging, a taut, flat stomach. Her attention locked onto him, mouth running dry, pulses starting to race.

'You make me feel like an exhibitionist,' Leo murmured with vibrant amusement.

Angie lowered her lashes, cheeks on fire. 'You've never been shy,' she breathed unevenly.

Leo laughed softly and shed the rest of his clothing. He was hugely aroused, supremely unconcerned by the fact. Angie tensed, suddenly desperately shy of him and aware of his virile masculinity with every skin-cell in her taut body.

'Come here...' He eased her to him, sliding a long, lean, darkly haired thigh between hers as he leant over her, all male in his dominance, and circled her lips teasingly with his. Angie stopped breathing. He nibbled at her full lower lip and she gave a little jump, the coil of wicked anticipation within her twisting ever tighter. He shifted sinuously over her and let the tip of his tongue dip erotically between her lips, making her shudder.

'Leo...'

'Patience, *pethi mou*... I've waited a very long time for this, and I intend to savour every moment,' Leo breathed huskily.

And then he crushed her soft mouth under his until every sense swam and she closed her arms round him in a sudden, convulsive movement.

Leo raised his head. 'That's better,' he told her, angling back from her to flick loose the front-fastening bra, baring her full breasts for his perusal.

He ran a caressing fingertip over one achingly erect rosy nipple, and a choked little sound broke in the back of Angie's throat. Leo surveyed her with immense satisfaction and dropped his dark head to torment that sensitive peak with his mouth. Frantic heat sprang up low in her stomach. Heartbeat hammering, Angie twisted beneath him, her fingers biting into his smooth brown back and then sweeping up to lace tightly into his thick, glossy hair instead.

'You're so beautiful,' Leo murmured intently, shaping her pouting breasts with reverent hands, letting his tongue flick sensually over the shamelessly engorged tips.

Clenching her teeth, Angie squirmed in tortured excitement. She gasped and struggled for every breath as waves of sensation thrummed through her. Then he let his teeth graze her swollen, straining flesh, and her hips rose and she moaned out loud in pure torment.

Leo stared down at her, golden eyes blazing, a fevered line of colour over his hard cheekbones. 'When you're out of control,' he confessed raggedly, 'it drives me wild.'

'I want you…' she gasped. 'I want you *so* much it hurts!'

Leo expelled his breath in a shaken hiss and, arching over her, almost crushed her beneath his full weight, his tongue plunging with explicit, driving need into the moist interior of her mouth over and over again.

'Am I being too rough?' he asked thickly.

'Oh, no…' Angie mumbled when she could catch her breath, reaching up an unsteady hand to touch his beautiful mouth, rubbing her fingers along that anxiously tensed line, a desperate tide of love overwhelming her.

Knotting a possessive hand into her tumbled hair, he smiled wolfishly down at her and smoothly disposed of the fragile barrier of silk and lace still encircling her hips. 'You're my woman…and I need to possess you so badly, I *ache*.'

Sending a sure hand skimming through the damp cluster of pale curls at the apex of her trembling thighs, he delicately traced the swollen, moist centre of her. Angie jerked, a moan of anguished need betraying her. Leo watched her with hungry appreciation, skilful fingers finding the most sensitive place of all and playing there until she was frantic with mindless, whimpering pleasure.

'Leo…*please*,' she begged, her whole body straining up to him.

He came over her in one strong movement and entered her yielding softness with a shuddering groan of raw satisfaction. The sensation surpassed her every expectation. He had only begun and her heart was banging wildly against her ribcage, making her weak with sheer over-excitement. Every screaming nerve was centred on his slow, powerful invasion, her passion-glazed eyes welded to the fierce control etched in his taut features.

'Leo...' she cried achingly. *'Leo!'*

And then he moved, thrusting deep into the heart of her. The power of speech was wrenched from her by the most shattering surge of physical pleasure. He felt so incredibly good, and she felt so deliciously possessed, she surrendered herself utterly. He drove into her with hard, rhythmic force. She cried out in strangled ecstasy and clung while the fierce ache of hunger surged higher and higher until, uncontrolled and out of her mind with excitement, she hit an electrifying starburst of sensation and fell over the edge into heaven.

She didn't float back to earth again either. Leo was holding her so close when she opened her dazed eyes, a breath of fresh air couldn't have got between their damp, hot bodies, and that felt like heaven too.

'May I continue?' Leo enquired raggedly.

Her lashes fluttered and then she registered that he was *still...*

'Oh...' she said guiltily, face burning as he lifted himself up to gaze down at her.

Glittering dark eyes vibrantly amused, Leo murmured forgivingly, 'You lasted a whole three minutes...that has to be some kind of record.'

In the middle of the night, Angie put on the light and watched Leo sleep for a good half-hour. All she wanted to do was feast her eyes on him. He was sprawled on his stomach, black hair tousled, lashes down like ebony silk fans, jawline blue-shadowed, a lot of rather embarrassing scratches scoring his once flawless back and one long, lean thigh partially exposed by the tangled sheet. Even sleeping, he was so gorgeous, it was the most appalling struggle for Angie not to seek actual physical contact.

Feeling incredibly possessive, she covered him up as gently and carefully as she covered up Jake, and then she slid restively out of bed to tiptoe round, picking up their discarded clothes. She was so ecstatically happy, she couldn't sleep. Only one tiny cloud marred her horizon. It had taken until after midnight to exhaust him, but that wasn't the cloud. Indeed Angie couldn't think of anything more wonderful than Leo's insatiable need to subject her to endless pleasure.

He had been so passionate, so tender, everything she recalled from before…only this time around she was absolutely terrified of him guessing that she was still madly in love with him. 'Too intense'. That was precisely what had driven him away from her two and a half years ago. Leo might have talked a lot of impressive sounding twaddle about her having been too young, but Angie remained unconvinced.

In two days *she* would be Leo's wife. He didn't love her but, if Leo had it in him to love, he would love her by the time she was finished with him. She would sign that stupid pre-nuptial agreement thing he had mentioned and surely then he would appreciate that she wasn't a gold-digger? Aside from that, a little coolness, a little distance, indeed a little mystery ought to make her all the more desirable a wife in his eyes… Abstractedly she breathed in the scent of him from his discarded shirt, eyes starry as she plotted and planned.

Angie woke up in Leo's shirt, Jake bouncing on the bed, ice-cream stains round his chattering mouth. His dark eyes glowing, he told her about having breakfast with his father, visiting some park, playing on the swings and falling off the slide. A trouser leg was rolled up to display a chubby knee bearing a minuscule plaster, and a replay of the fall was suddenly enacted. Angie caught her over-excited toddler a split second before he nose-dived off the bed in his enthusiasm.

'Go wash,' he announced importantly, sliding out of her arms again like an eel to scramble back down onto the carpet and race back to the door. 'Daddy say go wash.'

Angie sprang out of bed to give chase, but was drawn up at the bedroom door when she saw Harriet gather him up. 'I'll see to him,' the older woman said cheerfully. 'He'll need a change of clothes before he goes out.'

Angie had a shower and put on a slim black wool dress, scrubbing at her cheeks in the mirror to give herself some colour. A whole box of cosmetics, that was what she needed, she decided sunnily.

She walked down the stairs, careful in her high heels, not yet used to wearing them again. The library door was ajar and she could hear Leo speaking, so she hung back in case he had someone with him.

'There *is* no risk...' he was murmuring with audible amusement. 'But I still won't feel safe until I get that ring on her finger...no, I can't meet up with you beforehand...I don't want her to suspect what I'm up to.' His dark, deep drawl dropped even lower in pitch. 'Marisa, you're tremendous...'

Transfixed to the spot, Angie strained feverishly close to the door to hear what he was saying next, and distinctly heard a roughened reference to 'any sort of bed at all as long as it takes two', and then, in a very husky, sexy whisper, 'You're embarrassing me'...

Leo...*embarrassed*? Leo who didn't have a self-conscious bone in his body? Angie shuddered, perspiration dampening her upper lip as she jerked away from the door and shot across the hall into the drawing room opposite. He needn't worry about being embarrassed, she thought. He should worry about living to breathe another day!

CHAPTER TEN

SICK with shock at what she had overheard, Angie crept over to a chair and dropped down into it to stare into space. Leo and Marisa Laurence. Only two days before he married Angie, Leo was indulging in the sort of sexually suggestive dialogue which only lovers shared. After last night, how *could* Leo betray her trust to such an extent?

Unable to sit still, her sensitive stomach still turning somersaults, Angie got up again. Her mind was the most terrifying blank. All she was conscious of was the shattering pain of her own disbelief. And then she questioned even that sensation, for where had she ever got the idea that Leo would be faithful? She had been outrageously naive. An awful lot of men—and rich men in particular—were serial adulterers!

She fumbled to recall exactly what she had overheard. Leo wasn't prepared to meet up with Marisa before the wedding in case his bride-to-be got suspicious. He had also said that he wouldn't feel safe until that ring was on her finger. Some chance of that *now,* Angie reflected in agony. But, of course, Leo didn't want to upset the apple cart at present. He had a lot to lose if the wedding didn't go ahead.

When had she allowed herself to forget that Leo was marrying her only to gain legal rights over his son? As she abruptly recalled that pre-nuptial agreement he had mentioned, Angie's blood ran cold. Leo evidently planned to continue his affair with Marisa. Concerned that his extra-marital activities might provoke Angie into demanding a divorce, Leo would naturally seek to safeguard his wealth. Her pounding head ached. She blinked, breathed in deep. Her imagination was getting out of hand...

Leo *loved* Jake. Leo had to know that if there was a divorce and he tried to fight her for custody of their son it would be Jake who would suffer most. No, she wasn't dealing with some Machiavellian plan to steal her son away from her, she decided. Her sagging shoulders straightened. Her beautiful face clenched with sudden fury. She was dealing with a louse who had blithely assumed that he could be an unfaithful husband, a louse who would find out the hard way that if he put one toe out of line she would make him pay for it in spades!

Angie folded her arms, ramming back her pain with fierce determination. Oh, yes, she could confront Leo and refuse to marry him, and where would that leave her and her son? Leo's wealth would still put him in the driver's seat. He would have to support them. She would have to put up with him visiting for Jake's sake. She might even have to tolerate Marisa Laurence as her son's stepmother. No, marrying Leo would give her equality and a certain amount of power. Flouncing off in a huff would only reduce her to the level of being his dependant...wouldn't it?

'What's wrong?' Leo enquired with a startled frown when she pulled away from the light arm he had dropped round her shoulders as they left the town house.

'Nothing,' Angie said flatly.

'Look, there's obviously something wrong,' Leo stated with conviction in Harrods when Angie kept on behaving as if he was stalking them.

'Maybe I'm having a bad hair day,' she said frigidly.

With Harriet in restrictive tow, personal dialogue of any length was all but impossible. While everyone else ate their lunch, Angie enjoyed several glasses of wine on an empty stomach, grimly conscious of Leo's brooding frustration.

They had spent several hours in Harrods. Angie had resisted any suggestion that she might want to look at wedding dresses. But Jake was now in possession of a wardrobe large enough to clothe three little boys because, when it came to his son, Leo had no sense of proportion. He had also fully borne out Angie's every expectation in the toy department, and had gone on to hit Hamleys with unquenched enthusiasm.

But Angie had lurched at frightening speed from rage to misery to the kind of sick, despairing jealousy and pain that pooled like poison inside her. She had reached the stage where one minute she was convinced she could still marry Leo and happily make his life hell by policing his every movement, but the next she was convinced that she couldn't go through with the wedding under any circumstances.

In fact her emotions were in full and very dangerous control of her by the time the helicopter circled over Deveraux Court and made a neat landing on the pad to the west of the house. It was late afternoon, and the icy temperatures had finally borne out their wintry promise. It was starting to snow.

'Snow...' Jake gasped ecstatically as the first fat, fluffy flakes drifted slowly down. He raced across the gravel frontage of the house, twisting and turning like a miniature dervish as he tried to catch them.

Leo surveyed Angie. Angie watched their son as if his innocent wonder and joy were a tragedy of the biggest order. How *could* she deprive Jake of the father he already adored? Security, love, two parents. Those were the things which her son needed most...

The Great Hall was dominated by the Christmas tree. The Scots pine now glittered and glowed with gold and silver decorations and candle-shaped lights.

'I'm the sort of woman who would hack your designer suits into tiny shreds if you were ever unfaithful,' Angie delivered chattily to Leo as she slid out of her coat.

Having been momentarily engaged in watching their son trot off with both his grandfathers in keen pursuit, Leo's arrogant dark head whipped back round to her. Angie had the pleasure of seeing him utterly frozen to the spot, bold dark eyes incredulous.

Her smile was colder than the snowy peaks of the Himalayas as she climbed the stairs. 'I'm the sort of woman who would tell the whole story, with the inclusion of every minute and dirty detail, to the Press.'

'Angie—?'

'I'm the sort of woman who would rip you off for every penny you've got if you betrayed me,' Angie slung at him in warning from the minstrel's gallery. 'And I would be the sort of ex-wife who would feature only in your worst nightmares. I would be unreasonable, manipulative, demanding and just downright nasty!'

'What the hell is the matter with you?' Leo demanded not quite steadily as he strode up the stairs after her, taking them two at a time. 'Apart from rather too much wine...'

Angie stiffened, eyes flashing. 'I just thought you should know what you're getting into *before* you marry me. If I ever had cause to doubt your loyalty, I would hold spite and pursue vengeance until the day I died!'

'You're heading in the wrong direction.'

'No, I'm not,' Angie muttered tightly. 'While you are considering your options, I will be sleeping in the Chinese bedroom.'

'So I'll visit,' Leo delivered cheerfully.

In disbelief, Angie focused on the amusement flashing across his lean, strong face, shaken even in the mood she was in by the raw charisma he possessed. 'No way!'

Drew, looking rakish with a patch over one eye, strolled down the corridor towards them with his arm ostentatiously draped round a small, curvaceous brunette with smiling green eyes. 'This is Tally,' he announced.

'Hi...I'm Angie,' Angie managed to say, and then she walked on, only hesitating long enough to throw over her shoulder, 'And by the way, Leo, I will not be signing any pre-nuptial agreement!'

She closed the bedroom door behind her. A split second later, Leo thrust it open. No longer did he look amused. 'Drew and Tally heard that last crack,' he drawled in stark reproof.

Embarrassed by the rebuke, Angie shrugged jerkily, tears thickening her throat. 'Why should that worry you? Mr Sensitive you're not,' she condemned. 'As for that agreement, if you expect me to take *you* on trust, I expect you to take *me* on trust too.'

Lounging back against the door with innate grace, Leo studied her with measuring dark eyes. Infuriatingly he said nothing.

'After all, you've already made it clear that this is a marriage of convenience for our son's sake,' Angie continued doggedly. 'And maybe I'm not too sure of the kind of treatment I can expect to receive after the wedding.'

'When have I ever given you cause to question my sincerity?' Leo demanded with level bite.

Angie spun away and breathed in deep, hands knotting together. 'Someone told me that you were heavily involved with Marisa Laurence until very recently.'

'So *that* is what this is all about...'

Angie turned back to him, very pale and taut.

Exasperation had set Leo's hard facial bones. 'Marisa and I have been close friends for years. In fact, it's Marisa you have to thank for the soft toys and the clothes that were acquired for Jake the day you left the Dicksons'.'

'Close friends?' Angie repeated with tense, frowning uncertainty.

'With never a spark of anything sexual because there was never a spark even to begin with for either of us,' Leo supplied very drily. 'Marisa *is* heavily involved, however—not with me but with an environmental scientist who's been working abroad for the past year. Marisa stayed in the UK because she has a business to run.'

Angie stared at him with wide eyes, and then she reddened fiercely. There was something so very deflating and convincing about Leo's cool, incisive gaze and sardonic intonation.

'The "someone" who talked was Drew, right?' Leo prompted in derisive continuance. 'He doesn't miss a trick when it comes to causing trouble. But it's you I'm disappointed in, Angie. You talk about trust, and yet you couldn't bring yourself to just come right out and ask me about Marisa—'

'You're saying it's a platonic relationship...yet you wouldn't accept that same explanation from me—'

'Drew wanted you. The situation was different.' Leo wasn't yielding an inch. He opened the door again, his strong features harshly set.

Angie nibbled anxiously at her lower lip. 'Leo...I heard you on the phone to Marisa this morning and it didn't sound like a purely friendly conversation—but possibly I misunderstood,' she muttered in an increasing rush. 'Only you were talking about not wanting me to suspect what you were up to, not being willing to meet her before the wedding...'

'You'll understand after the wedding. Until then I'm afraid you'll have to take me on trust,' Leo imparted with distinct irony as he closed the door.

Angie was so worked up she burst into floods of tears. Evidently she had got herself into a state over nothing. But why the reference to a bed? A joke, a flirtatious innuendo between old friends? Leo had been so cool, calm and superior. But she wondered how he might have reacted had he eavesdropped on a similar one-sided dialogue. But she could answer that question for herself—Leo would have immediately confronted her. Openly and honestly.

Her luggage arrived and a maid appeared to do the unpacking. Angie went off in search of Leo, only to discover that he had taken Jake down to the stables with him. Her father reminded her that it was the staff party that evening. That meant that the family would be dining out and returning late.

A knock sounded on the bedroom door as Angie was trying to decide what to wear.

It was Drew. Without invitation, he made himself carelessly at home on the side of the bed.

'What do you want?' Angie enquired thinly.

He grimaced. 'I guess I owe you an apology for what I did two years ago.'

'Fine…is there anything else?'

Drew gave her a reproachful look. 'I was rather nasty the other night, but I wasn't expecting to find you here and, frankly, it was one of the worst nights of my life!'

'Yes,' Angie allowed grudgingly, thinking of the many shocks Drew had been dealt at the dinner table. 'I suppose it was. But where *did* you get the strange idea that Leo was almost on the brink of marriage with Marisa?'

Drew went red and evaded her eyes. 'So I exaggerated a bit—'

'A *bit*?' Angie derided grimly.

'OK…so I knew they were just friends. It just riled me, seeing you with Leo again,' he admitted rather rawly. 'I hate the way he always seems to get what he wants. But Tally thinks that I did a rotten thing keeping the two of you apart.'

'You didn't keep us apart. Leo had already scrubbed me out of his life.'

Drew groaned. 'Well, who can say how it would've turned out? But Leo *did* land back here a few weeks later, expecting you to be sitting waiting like faithful Penelope even though he'd ditched you…and you weren't; you were painting the town red with *me*!'

Angie was frowning. 'What are you talking about?'

'I could've been noble and stepped back and made it clear that there was nothing heavy between us, but I'm not noble and I *didn't*. Actually, I revelled in the knowledge that Leo wanted you back and thought he had missed the boat.'

'That time he visited…he wanted me back?' Angie whispered unevenly. 'Did he tell you that?'

Drew rolled his eyes. 'Angie…can you really see Leo confiding in me?'

'No…but you said—'

'It was obvious that you were the only reason he came here. He flew straight back to Athens first thing the next morning.' Drew sighed as he read the devastated look in her eyes. 'He was his own worst enemy, Angie. He could've put his cards on the table then and given you a chance…'

Angie spun her head defensively away, her throat thickening as she recalled Leo approaching her when she had come home at the end of that evening. 'He did try to talk to me…but I wasn't really paying the right sort of attention.'

'At the time I thought it was hilarious,' Drew confided wryly. 'Everybody *but* Leo knew that you had always been crazy about him.'

The door opened without a warning knock. Leo froze on the threshold. Drew uttered a very rude word in his dismay. Angie's tear-filled eyes encountered a look as aggressive as an attack in Leo's glittering dark gaze.

'This is as close as I ever got to Angie's bed…honest it is,' Drew quipped with a distinctly strained laugh. 'For heaven's sake, Leo…lighten up before you give me a heart attack!'

Leo swung on his heel and strode off down the corridor. Angie made a move to follow him. Drew stepped in her path. 'Give me a chance to get well out of the way first,' he said wryly. 'I do not want to be involved in this round.

I've got Tally now, and, although you're still a remarkable eyeful, you're definitely more Leo's style. I'm not into throbbing passion and high drama, but the pair of you appear to thrive on them!'

As soon as Drew was gone, Angie splashed her face with cold water. Leo had come back specifically to see her on that flying visit to the Court two years ago... Dear heaven, could that be true? And had she, in her bitter pride and driving need to appear untouched by his rejection, been her own worst enemy too? The suspicion savaged her.

'Your presence has a wondrously enlivening effect on Leo,' Wallace remarked when she went to collect Jake from the drawing room. 'I know my grandson as a serious, rational and even-tempered man. You make him do extraordinary things.'

'Such as?'

Wallace gave her a sardonic smile. 'Sneaking into his own home like a cat burglar with roses and pink champagne. He hates flowers...he hates champagne. Such as storming out like a thundercloud, leaping into his Ferrari and driving off...'

Angie had turned pink. 'Leo's gone out?'

His grandfather nodded. Angie swallowed hard and took Jake to have his tea. Her son's energy level was flagging fast. He was half-asleep when she lifted him out of the high chair, and in no state for a bath. Gently slotting him into his pyjamas, she put him to bed. Drew's girlfriend, Tally, came in to take a peek at him.

They parted outside Angie's bedroom door, having shared a thorough discussion of what each of them planned to wear that night, although the brunette had done most of the talking. Angie was finding it hard to concentrate because all the time she was wondering when Leo would get back, *if* Leo was planning to come back and even if there would be a wedding—for avoiding confrontation was not a characteristic that she was used to Leo displaying.

She owed him a full explanation about Drew. She had never attempted to explain that relationship in a way which would make sense to Leo. So naturally he was still uneasy. His cousin was a part of his family, and likely to be around now on a regular basis. All Leo had ever asked her for was the truth, but she had been too proud to give him it.

Was the intensity of her relief written across her face when she entered the drawing room and found Leo there? He skimmed a narrowed glance over her jade-green dress and light jacket. Angie stared back at him helplessly, her pupils dilating, her breath running out in her throat. His hair still damp and slightly curly from the shower, he was wearing a casual but incredibly elegant dark suit with a silver-grey sweater. He looked devastatingly sexy in the way only a very masculine man could.

'Shall we go?' he suggested to the room at large, and then he flicked a glance at Angie. 'I presume you're putting on your coat?'

She would have a chance to talk to him in the car, she assumed. But it was not to be. All five of them piled into the back of the limousine. It was a short drive to the country house hotel which had the only restaurant in the district Wallace was prepared to patronise. Angie was seething with desperation to get Leo on his own by the time they walked into the hotel. She closed a hand round his sleeve and leant up to whisper, 'Leo—'

'This is not the place, Angie,' he said very drily.

Mortified, Angie withdrew her hand. She watched him over dinner. Although the winter chill never ebbed from his spectacular dark eyes, he laughed and he chatted with an easy social dexterity she was quite incapable of emulating. Wallace was the life and soul of the party.

'Leo behaving badly...I love it,' Drew murmured at one point under cover of the conversation.

Angie looked up as a group of people stopped by their table to exchange greetings with Leo. A tiny, svelte blonde with huge blue eyes studied her intently and then smiled at her. She extended her hand. 'I don't think we've ever been formally introduced, Angie.'

'Marisa...' Angie's smile was strained as she stood up, towering over the other woman and feeling absolutely huge.

'I'm so pleased for you both,' Marisa confided with the kind of warm and deep sincerity that even the Wicked Witch of the West couldn't have doubted.

'Lovely woman,' Wallace commented as she moved off again. 'It's a mystery to me why she's not married. This career woman nonsense, I expect...owns one of those twee decorating outfits, doesn't she?'

'An interior design consultancy that's worth several million,' Leo responded.

'*Never*...' Wallace ejaculated in healthy astonishment.

Angie was shrinking. Marisa was little, gorgeous to look at, successful in business and genuinely nice. She was convinced that Leo had to be comparing them to *her* detriment. Tally and Drew got up to dance. Wallace was hailed by an old gentleman sitting at a nearby table and he went over to socialise. Leo lounged back in his chair and surveyed Angie in silence.

'You're angry with me—'

Leo rose abruptly from his seat. 'Let's get some fresh air...'

'Leo... Drew came to my room to apologise for all the things he's done,' she muttered as he fed her into her coat with astonishingly gentle hands in the foyer.

'You were crying,' he gritted.

Angie sucked in a deep, anxious breath. 'I was in love with you two and a half years ago.'

'I know...' Leo said flatly, swinging open the door and

walking her into the still white world beyond. 'I am not stupid.'

Silenced by that assurance, Angie bit the soft underside of her lower lip, tasted blood and shivered in the cold, crisp air.

'But you were very young,' Leo murmured in driven addition. 'It was perfectly possible that in the space of a few weeks you had fallen out of love with me and into love with him.'

'But I didn't...and Drew knew right from the start that I loved you—'

'You *told* him?' Leo shot her a startled glance and then he groaned. 'For the first time in my life I feel sorry for my cousin.'

'That's why we were only ever friends.'

'*Cristos*...no wonder he hit the bottle so hard while he was with you! To have you and yet *not* have you,' Leo breathed with a stark shudder. 'I could not have borne a relationship like that.'

'I talked about you all the time as well,' Angie confided guiltily. 'But I honestly *didn't* know how he felt about me. And this evening something he said upset me and that's why I was crying. He said...he said that time you flew over for twenty-four hours—he said that he thought you wanted me back—'

'I *did*,' Leo confirmed, closing a strong arm round her and pulling her close as they walked down the well-lit path under the white, frosted silhouette of the trees.

'So why did you ditch me in the first place, then?' Angie demanded strickenly, her lovely face convulsing with the strength of her emotions.

Leo stilled and rested his hands on her quivering shoulders. His brilliant dark eyes were full of pain and regret. 'I needed time away from you to work out what was going on inside my own head. I wasn't happy with Petrina, but I *chose* her...how could I have any faith in my own judgement after one weekend with you? What room did I have to even explore my feelings *with* you when both our families would've been justly outraged by the level of intimacy we had already enjoyed?'

'Are you s-saying that you thought you m-might be in love with me then?' Angie framed so shakily she could hardly get the words out.

'I was afraid it was only an infatuation which wouldn't last on my side…and you were so vulnerable. I *had* to leave, and I couldn't make you any promises. I didn't know if I would come back to you.'

'You could've told me the truth,' Angie condemned unevenly. 'You could've asked me to wait—'

Leo vented a harsh laugh. 'I was arrogant enough to believe that I didn't *have* to ask. I wasn't prepared for you to take up with Drew, but I recalled enough of my own teenage experiences to know that nothing is more fickle and fleeting than the emotions of youth. You seemed happy with him—'

'Where were your eyes?' Angie gulped, tears clogging up her throat. 'I was *miserable*.'

'I was very angry… Strange as it may seem, I felt that you were the one who had made a fool out of me. I had spent six weeks wrestling with my desire for you,' he admitted rawly. 'And there you were, prancing about happily with my cousin. I wanted to kill you, but I told myself I had had a narrow escape from making an even bigger ass of myself.'

'I didn't w-want you to know how much you'd hurt me.'

'Ditto…' Leo said roughly half under his breath, and he gathered her close, crushing her into his arms and then framing her tear-stained face with his hands to look down at her, bold dark eyes intense and possessive. 'And now I've got you back in my arms I'm never letting go of you again.'

His hungry mouth was cool on hers and then hot…

hot…hot, the taste and the scent of him and the hard strength of his powerful physique filling her with electrifying excitement. She went pliant and clung. Leo needed no further encouragement. Wallace coughed unnoticed from the hotel steps. That kiss went on and on and on until Drew wolf-whistled from the limousine which had drawn up on the other side of the snowy verge.

Angie didn't remember the drive back to the Court. It meant so much to her that Leo had come back for her after that weekend, and she didn't know whether she was on her head or her heels. She floated back into the house, tucked under Leo's arm, and drank a toast to Christmas with him as the staff gathered in the Great Hall, laughing and chatting and full of seasonal spirit after their own evening of festivities. Leo gave a wonderful speech about how much he appreciated everyone's hard work. Angie watched him with the exclusive attention of a woman in love.

They got one foot towards the stairs. The head groom broke breathlessly through the thinning knots of the departing staff, his wrinkled face troubled. 'I'm afraid that little mare looks like she's going to deliver early, sir. I've phoned for the vet but he's on another call, and with it being her first foal…'

'It's OK…I'll come and take a look at her.' Leo gave Angie a rueful look. 'Don't wait up for me,' he advised.

'I could come with you…'

Leo frowned and shook his head with decision. 'No point in both of us going without a night's sleep.'

Angie went to bed alone, feeling hurt. She might not be as skilled or as experienced as Leo was with horses, but it certainly wouldn't have been the first foal she had helped to deliver. As a teenager she had spent all her free time down at the stables. But then Leo didn't feel any need to have her hovering round him *all* the time, did he? Only a man in love would have welcomed her company.

But two and a half years ago, given the time, the space

and the opportunity, Leo *might* have fallen in love with her. That was a bitter pill to swallow. But after he had seen her with Drew any fledgling feelings he had had for her had been destroyed. He had spent almost all the years since believing that she had slept with Drew, become pregnant with his cousin's child...not to mention believing that she was the household thief.

When he had come back into her life again, he had done so on Wallace's behalf alone, and initially he had been anything but pleased to find himself still attracted to her. But, being Leo, he had soon decided that the logical thing to do was to go to bed with her and get her out of his system, and he probably would have managed that feat, she conceded, growing steadily more wretched, had it not been for the fact that she was the mother of his son.

Any treacherous and insidious thought that she might reasonably lodge herself in Leo's bed and wait for his return was now soundly squashed, and even the memory of the thought a source of deep shame. Angie clutched a pillow miserably to herself. She would never throw herself at Leo again.

Angie's father brought her breakfast in bed the next morning. She sat up and practically snatched the tray from him. 'Dad!' she scolded in embarrassment. 'I don't want you waiting on me...it's not right!'

Samuel Brown chuckled. 'There are so many staff here now that I rarely get to lift anything heavier than the morning post. I wanted a word with you. Have you got a wedding dress yet?' he enquired anxiously. 'I suppose I'm a little late asking.'

'No, you're not.'

Smiling with relief at the news, he informed her that that was just as well because it was his duty to buy her one. These days, he told her proudly, he had a very healthy savings account. Before she knew where she was, he had organised her day for her. She was to make a shopping trip into Exeter with her stepmother and buy the best dress she could find. And what about presents? he asked. Had she bought presents for everyone? Her face fell a mile. He shook his greying head. 'So Leo doesn't think of everything.'

'It wouldn't even occur to Leo to suspect that I might be running round with less than five pounds in my purse...he couldn't imagine that level of penury— Gosh!' she exclaimed. 'You actually called him *Leo*!'

'I feel rather idiotic calling my future son-in-law anything else. As Wallace says, we have to move with the times unless we want to be written off as a couple of hidebound old fogies. But it's hard to break the habits of a lifetime.'

Apparently, Leo had spent the night in the stables, appeared for breakfast at seven and then gone to bed. The foal had been delivered successfully. But Angie was deprived of even a view of Leo before she left the house.

It was the most frantic day. But Angie fell in love with a dress in the second shop they visited. It had a stand-up Elizabethan-style beaded collar, a tightly fitting bodice and a lowish neckline, and it was the most beautiful shade of ivory. Angie looked in the mirror and saw a medieval princess gazing romantically back at her, and that was that.

Buying Christmas presents was the greater challenge. A book on modern manners for her father, another book—but a humorous one—for Wallace. For Drew cigars and for Tally a silk scarf. She bought a blouse for Emily while her stepmother was in a coffee shop. And then she came to Leo—Leo, a male who already had everything right down to a solid gold pocket knife and Turnbull and Asser shirts inscribed with his initials. She dragged her stepmother from shop to shop, and then daringly settled for another book— love poems. There was always the hope that inspiration might lead to change.

It was dark when they got back to the Court, but the great house sat with blazing, light-filled and welcoming windows of warmth, surrounded by the snow. A rather unusual snowman now adorned the lawn. He wore a black trilby, a false beard and sunglasses.

Angie, having been deprived of Leo for an entire day, was now indecently eager to see him again. She sped into the Great Hall, attention landing on Drew and Tally, who were standing by the log fire, both of them looking so embarrassingly flushed and tousled that she did the decent thing and pretended not to have noticed them.

'Where's Leo?' she asked her father, who was coming down the stairs.

Samuel Brown frowned in surprise. 'Do you know, I haven't a clue.'

'He said he had some last-minute shopping to do,' Drew delivered surreptitiously, straightening his rumpled sweater.

'Took the hump at you disappearing all day, I shouldn't wonder,' Wallace volunteered when Angie went into the drawing room. 'He got up at lunchtime, built a snowman for Jake and then spent the rest of the afternoon pacing by the window like a great prat! I couldn't get a sensible word out of him.'

'Oh...' Angie had extreme difficulty picturing Leo behaving like a 'great prat', and could only assume that his grandfather was exaggerating. Wallace then went on to complain about Drew and Tally canoodling in every corner like demented turtle doves and, shaking his head, returned to his book. 'Better company to be had between these pages.'

Her father was waiting for her when she emerged. 'Emily and I would like you to spend this last night with us in the flat,' he told her hopefully. 'It'll not be a chance we ever have again. Of course, if you have other plans...'

'No, I haven't.' But Angie turned a deep, guilty pink because she had been ready to lurk in the neighbourhood of the front door to wait for Leo. She bit her lip. 'That's a lovely idea…I'll come down as soon as Jake's settled for the night.'

Yes, you were going to play it cool with Leo, not behave like an adoring, desperate doormat, she scolded herself.

Eleven o'clock found her ensconced in the narrow bed in her father and stepmother's spare room. Even though it was unrecognisable as the room she had once slept in, it was rather touchingly adorned with the childhood mementos and books she had brought to the Court with her at thirteen. They had kept a place for her and that warmed her heart, but it didn't stop her tossing and turning and wishing she were with Leo. Tomorrow was Christmas Eve and her wedding day, and she really couldn't yet believe that. It was also her twenty-second birthday…but, it being so close to Christmas, nobody had ever paid much heed to it, so Angie never had either.

A soft knock sounded on the window-pane. As the bed was right up against the window, Angie almost jumped out of her skin. She rolled over onto her stomach and sat up, and saw Leo in the moonlight. She opened the window without hesitation.

'Are you coming out…or am I coming in?'

Angie scrambled barefoot over the window-sill, only to give a stifled squeal when the soles of her feet hit snow. Leo whipped off his coat, wrapped her in it and lifted her into his arms. She didn't get the chance to ask where they were going because he was so busy kissing her. She clutched at him as if they had been apart a month, head swirling and heat infiltrating every chilled inch of her responsive body.

Leo lowered her carefully down onto the window-ledge and lifted his head, breathing in deep and audibly.

It took Angie longer to recover. 'Why were you pacing the floor when I was out today?' she gasped.

'Because you were in a car...and it was in weather like this that Petrina and Jenny went off the road,' he divulged tautly.

'Oh, hell, Leo...I never even *thought*,' Angie sighed, arms fastening even tighter round him as she hugged him close in consolation.

Broad shoulders shrugged beneath her arms. 'It was stupid of me...but lightning can strike twice in the same place, *pethi mou*. That's why I went out. Waiting for you was driving me crazy.'

Angie rested her head on his shoulder, blissfully drawing in the reassuring scent of him. He had been worried sick about her. A wave of overpowering love engulfed her, and she recalled his miserable marriage and his disillusionment and she decided to be generous. 'I'll sign that pre-nuptial whatsit if you like,' she offered.

Leo groaned in the circle of her arms. 'That was a joke that rebounded on me...I had no intention of demanding that you sign any such agreement. I was simply paying you back for pretending that you were a gold-digger on the make two years ago.'

Angie jerked and lifted her head, eyes wide. 'Paying me back?'

Leo studied her with rueful amusement. 'That very first night I saw you again, you told me that you had been very much in love with your son's father...'

Angie's soft mouth dropped open.

'And you said it with such fire...you threw it in my face with relish. When I realised Jake was mine, I recalled that conversation and I finally got the answer to a question that had plagued me for a very long time.'

'The problem plagued me even longer,' Angie confided. 'I've had my eye on you since I was thirteen.'

'Angie...Angie,' Leo framed with helpless amusement.

'I set out to get you any way I could...I wanted to make up for Jenny,' she said chokily. 'It was so stupid.'

'No, it wasn't…and you've blessed me with a beautiful child who was conceived in love.' With a ragged sigh, Leo scooped her back off the ledge and planted her firmly back on the bed beyond. 'And since I don't want our next child to be conceived outdoors I think I'll say goodnight, *pethi mou.*'

Dizzily, Angie watched the moonlight twirling little circles on the ceiling. She remembered him saying how tremendous he felt the day he'd asked her to marry him. Now she wondered if that had related to her as well as Jake. She went to sleep with a blitzed smile on her face. He might not be romantic but he was very sexy…

In the little country church in the village, Leo waited at the altar. Drew looked unusually serious in his role of best man, and Angie smiled because she hadn't expected to see Drew in that role. She drifted down the aisle on her father's arm, conscious with every step that Leo's dark golden eyes were welded to her with the most flattering degree of intensity.

Every word of the marriage service which followed seemed to have special meaning for her. When they exchanged rings, Leo retained a grip on her hand. Jake plonked himself between them as they drove back to the Court. Then the lure of the flowers in his mother's hair proved to be too much of a temptation and Leo had to distract him. Angie was incapable of anything other than studying her ring and her new husband.

A smart photographer and his assistant awaited them back at the Court. After being made to pose just about everywhere but at the top of the Christmas tree alongside the angel, Angie gave Leo a pleading look of frustration.

'I've never had a photograph of you…don't you realise that?' he countered.

'He's going to sit in his big fancy office with lots of

photos of you so that he can get through the day without you,' Drew mocked.

Angie's heart blossomed with hope.

'I hope you won't mind that we're leaving you now,' Leo announced at the end of the indoor photographic session, entwining Angie's fingers with his and leading her to the door.

'Where are we going?' Angie demanded.

A gleaming open-topped carriage complete with a coachman and two horses sat outside waiting. Poleaxed by the sight, Angie allowed herself to be hustled out and handed up. Leo curved her up against him. 'Don't ask any more questions. Just wait and see.'

The horses trotted not down the drive but round to the back of the house, and stopped at the stable block. Leo helped her down from the carriage and swept her over to one of the stalls. 'Happy birthday,' he said with quiet pride. 'The mare's called Reba and the filly hasn't got a name yet. They're yours.'

Angie gazed, dumbstruck, at the silver-grey Arab mare and her long-legged, gawky but beautiful baby. 'Nobody bothers about my birthday.'

'I do,' Leo asserted. 'What will you call the filly?'

'Joy,' Angie told him dizzily.

From the stables, the carriage turned down one of the lanes which criss-crossed the estate, passing through the woods and then climbing. Angie was in a daze.

'Close your eyes,' Leo told her.

The horses came to a halt a few minutes later, and this time Leo simply lifted her up into his arms. Angie tried to peek. He kissed her, and she always closed her eyes when Leo kissed her. When he set her down, she wasn't quite sure she was still earthbound and, when her lashes lifted, she was even less sure because she appeared to be standing inside the Folly, and it had been transformed again.

Only this time the Folly had been transformed with striking warmth, colour and taste. Angie's stunned gaze slowly drifted over the crackling fire in the polished grate, the soft, deep carpet, sofas, rugs and throws, the wonderful little Christmas tree, and a giant lump formed in her throat.

'This is what I didn't want you to suspect I was up to.'

'Oh, Leo,' she gulped.

'Marisa pulled off a miracle for me. This is why I insisted on taking you up to London. I wanted this to be a surprise.'

Marisa and her interior design consultancy. Setting up the Folly for their wedding night had been the subject of that conversation.

'It is…' Angie said hoarsely. 'It's the most wonderful surprise anybody has ever given me.'

Leo turned her slowly round. 'It was the happiest weekend I ever had in my adult life,' he breathed tautly. 'And yet I walked away from what we had shared because I was so damned scared of making another mistake!'

Angie was seeing him through a fog of tears. 'I was only nineteen…I can't blame you for doubting that we could have a future.'

Leo drew her down onto the sofa by the fire. 'I started looking for you three months after you left the Court.'

'But why? At the time you thought I was expecting Drew's baby.'

'And he hadn't looked after you. I wanted to be sure you were all right because I blamed myself for what had happened with him. I had rejected you after giving you every reason to expect more of me,' Leo breathed with stark regret in his deep, dark voice. 'But I couldn't find you. If there was a trail to follow, it had gone cold by then.'

More tears clouded her vision at the thought of Leo looking for her without success when she would have so rejoiced in being found. For a moment, he held her so close she could hardly breathe.

'I kept the investigators at work, but more or less gave

up hope,' Leo confessed grimly. 'And then you registered to vote a couple of months ago and bingo—you were no longer lost.'

'A couple of months ago?'

'I asked for a full report on you before I informed Wallace. I knew everything down to your shoe size before I came knocking on that door. I even made sure that the Dicksons would be out,' Leo volunteered with raw discomfiture. 'I worked very hard at telling myself that finding you didn't mean anything personal to me after so long, but…'

'But?' Angie prodded anxiously.

'*Theos*…I was kidding myself. One look and all I wanted to do was gather you up in my arms and take you home with me.'

'But Jake stuck in your throat…'

'At first—not by the time we arrived at the Court. And then Drew arrived and things went haywire…or possibly I was the one who went haywire. All of a sudden, I didn't know which of us you might want, and I was terrified of losing you.'

'Leo…you could never lose me…you idiot,' she said shakily, rubbing one blunt cheekbone with caressing fingers. 'I love you like mad; don't you know that?'

'And did I wreck your self-esteem so much that you still can't tell when a man is wildly in love with you?' Leo enquired as he raised her upright, passed a long arm below her legs and carried her up the stone staircase.

'You played games, Leo.'

'You wouldn't admit that you loved me.'

'Why wouldn't *you*?'

'I tried to *show* you in every way I know,' he protested defensively. 'Couldn't you see how happy I was the day I asked you to marry me?'

'You told me, you didn't ask.'

'We'd already wasted so much time apart, and I just couldn't wait to make you mine.'

Angie focused on the candlelit upper room, and, primarily, the most gorgeous bed festooned in lace. 'Definitely big enough for two.'

'You heard that?' Leo exclaimed. '*Cristos*...no wonder you were suspicious! Marisa was teasing the life out of me—what sort of a bed? What sort of sheets did you like? I just gave her a free hand.'

'So what were you doing with Marisa that night until two in the morning?' Angie queried.

'I left her about eleven...then I drove around, thinking about you.'

Angie pushed a proprietorial hand through his thick black hair. 'So who was it you *were* dating? You did say you had a date that first night...'

'Protective fib,' Leo confessed cheerfully as he lowered her to the bed. 'I had a business dinner...I should've known I was a lost cause where you were concerned the minute I lied.'

Angie reached up and kissed him. Leo came down to her with smouldering dark eyes and a tender smile that turned her bones to water. 'I adore you, Mrs Demetrios,' he told her softly. 'And being romantic is no longer a major effort.'

Angie lay back with an ecstatic and quite shameless sigh of invitation. 'More children?' she offered as if she were holding out a lure.

Leo's smile was blinding. 'You're just so perfect for me.'

'I'm making you perfect for me,' Angie whispered blithely.

Clothes melted away like snow off a hot chimney. Sentences became increasingly disjointed and finally ebbed altogether as passion swept the two of them away in a joyous celebration of their love.

At six in the morning, they climbed out of bed and helped themselves to the supper they had ignored the night before.

Leo's pre-planning had been so exact that even a change of clothes awaited them both. Arms possessively wrapped round each other, aglow with mutual contentment, they walked up to the Court in the dark and discovered that even Jake was still fast asleep.

Angie's father had ensured that their son's presents were all sitting in readiness below the tree. So Angie and Leo exchanged presents. Angie received a whole host of items, and handed over her single gift in some mortification. When Leo went into whoops on opening that book of love poems, she mock-punched him in the ribs, and he pulled her down beneath him and stole her embarrassment with one passionate kiss that went on and on, and very nearly turned into something quite unsuitable for the Great Hall.

'"How do I love thee? Let me count the ways",' Leo then quoted from the much maligned book, beautiful dark eyes resting with slumbrous hunger and appreciation on Angie as she ripped off wrapping paper to get at her presents. 'Yes...I could get into that one.'

He brought Jake down in his pyjamas. Jake took one wide-eyed look at the toy car and had not the slightest interest in opening anything as pedestrian as a wrapped present. He careened about the ground floor in noisy ecstasy, and toot-tooted his determined way into Wallace's rooms. 'Ganpa...Ganpa!' he called.

Leo loosed a wicked laugh. 'The wonder of a small child at Christmas,' he roared. 'I bet Wallace is putting a pillow over his ears!'

'*Leo*...' Angie's cheeks burned as she tugged out a black lace bustier.

'The spirit of self-indulgence crept in occasionally...and you could model it after lunch.'

'I could put it on for lunch...'

'Put it on *for* lunch?' Leo was aghast.

'This *isn't* lingerie, Leo. This is an outer garment.'

'No way are you showing yourself in public in that!'

Angie laughed and stopped winding him up. 'Relax, Leo. My father would throw a table napkin round me if I exposed that much flesh.'

Ten minutes later she was still piling up gift after gift. Jewellery, the most vast box of cosmetics, another coat, a pile of books, a whole host of cute little things that she just knew Leo secretly considered naff. But he had bought them to please her all the same. 'Oh Leo...I only got you that one little book,' she moaned.

'Actually I did fantastically well this Christmas, *pethi mou*,' Leo confided with supreme satisfaction as he eased her back possessively into the strong circle of his arms. 'I got you...and I got Jake.'

Angie turned her mouth up blissfully under his. They didn't quite manage to merge.

'If there's likely to be any of that canoodling at this hour of the day, I shall go back to bed!' Wallace threatened.

Garbed in a rather magnificent crimson wool dressing gown, he seated himself in the chair nearest the fire. Angie's father, fully dressed and immaculate, placed himself behind the chair. Wallace twisted his head round and frowned. 'Oh, sit down, Sam, for heaven's sake! They've bubbled us, and you don't want to be standing around with that arthritic knee of yours. Right, where are my pressies?'

Take 2 bestselling love stories FREE

Plus get a FREE surprise gift!

Special Limited-Time Offer

Mail to Harlequin Reader Service®

3010 Walden Avenue
P.O. Box 1867
Buffalo, N.Y. 14240-1867

YES! Please send me 2 free Harlequin Presents® novels and my free surprise gift. Then send me 6 brand-new novels every month, which I will receive months before they appear in bookstores. Bill me at the low price of $3.12 each plus 25¢ delivery and applicable sales tax, if any*. That's the complete price, and a saving of over 10% off the cover prices—quite a bargain! I understand that accepting the books and gift places me under no obligation ever to buy any books. I can always return a shipment and cancel at any time. Even if I never buy another book from Harlequin, the 2 free books and the surprise gift are mine to keep forever.

106 HEN CH69

Name	(PLEASE PRINT)	
Address	Apt. No.	
City	State	Zip

This offer is limited to one order per household and not valid to present Harlequin Presents® subscribers. *Terms and prices are subject to change without notice. Sales tax applicable in N.Y.

UPRES-98 ©1990 Harlequin Enterprises Limited

Toast the special events in your life with Harlequin Presents®!

With the purchase of *two* Harlequin Presents® BIG EVENT books, you can send in for two sparkling plum-colored Wineglasses. A retail value of $19.95!

ACT NOW TO COLLECT
TWO BEAUTIFUL WINEGLASSES!

On the official proof-of-purchase coupon below, fill in your name, address and zip or postal code and send it, plus $2.99 U.S./$3.99 CAN. for postage and handling (check or money order—please do not send cash) payable to Harlequin Books, to: In the U.S.: 3010 Walden Avenue, P.O. Box 9077, Buffalo, N.Y. 14269-9077; In Canada: P.O. Box 609, Fort Erie, Ontario L2A 5X3. Please allow 4-6 weeks for delivery. Order your set of wineglasses now! Quantities are limited. Offer for the Plum Wineglasses expires December 31, 1998.

Harlequin Presents®—The Big Event! ✂

OFFICIAL PROOF OF PURCHASE

"Please send me my TWO Wineglasses"

Name: _____

Address: _____

City: _____

State/Prov.: _____ Zip/Postal Code: _____

Account Number: _____ **097 KGS CSA6 193-3**

HPBEPOP

◆ **HARLEQUIN®**
Makes any time special ™

Coming Next Month

HARLEQUIN PRESENTS®

THE BEST HAS JUST GOTTEN BETTER!

#1995 MARRIED BY CHRISTMAS Carole Mortimer
Lilli was mortified when she woke up in Patrick Devlin's bed!
He wasn't about to let her forget it, either. Patrick would
save her father's chain of hotels...if she married him—by
Christmas!

#1996 THE BRIDAL BED Helen Bianchin
(Do Not Disturb)
For her mother's wedding, Suzanne and her ex-fiancé, Sloan,
had to play the part of a happy, soon-to-marry couple! After
sharing a room—and a bed!—their pretend passion became
real...and another wedding was on the agenda!

#1997 BABY INCLUDED! Mary Lyons
(The Big Event!)
Lord Ratcliffe was delighted that Eloise had turned up at
his surprise birthday party. He'd always thought she
was an ordinary American tourist; but in fact she was an
international sex symbol...and secretly carrying his baby!

#1998 A HUSBAND'S PRICE Diana Hamilton
Six years ago when Adam and Claudia had split up, he'd left
a part of himself with her—a child. Now Adam's help comes
with a hefty price tag—that Claudia become his wife. Faced
with bankruptcy and a custody battle, Claudia has no
choice....

#1999 A NANNY FOR CHRISTMAS Sara Craven
(Nanny Wanted!)
Dominic Ashton thought Phoebe was a wonderful stand-in
mom for little Tara; it was a pity she couldn't stay longer.
But Phoebe had her reasons for going: if Dominic had
forgotten their first meeting years before, she certainly
hadn't!

#2000 MORGAN'S CHILD Anne Mather
(Harlequin Presents' 2000th title!)
Four years after the death of her husband in war-torn Africa,
Felicity Riker at last had a new man...a new life. Then she
heard that Morgan had been found *alive*...and that he was
on his was back to reclaim his long-lost wife....